WALT DISNEY'S

Annette

and the

MYSTERY AT SMUGGLERS' COVE

Authorized Edition featuring ANNETTE,
star of motion pictures and television

by
Doris Schroeder

Illustrated by
Nathalee Mode

NEW YORK

First Edition
1 2 3 4 5 6 7 8 9 10

Library of Congress Catalog Card Number on file.

ISBN 0-7868-4558-9
For more Disney Press fun, visit www.disneybooks.com

Contents

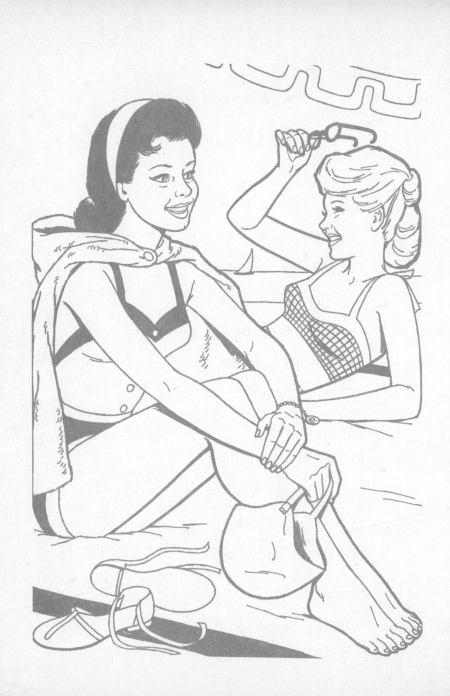

1
Annette's Little Joke

"Oh, dear!" Annette's pretty suntanned face had lost its usual cheery smile, and she sighed heavily. "Here it's practically the end of August and school vacation's almost over!"

Her friend and houseguest, Babs Gray, lifted her blond head from the adjoining beach mat and groaned. "Just when I was being so peaceful and contented, you had to remind me. School, ugh!" And she laid back down on her resting place under the red-striped beach umbrella.

Annette's dark eyes twinkled. "I'm sorry," she told Babs. "I didn't mean to spoil your nap." She sat hugging her knees and staring off at the wide expanse of the Pacific Ocean beyond the curving outline of the Laguna shore.

Half an hour earlier, when she and Babs had taken their morning swim, the ocean beyond the bay had been smooth. Now, the late morning breeze was making it choppy. Out on the horizon to the south some white clouds were slowly creeping up the sky. That usually meant there was a tropical storm on the coast of lower California, and little fragments of it were being blown north. Sometimes, but very seldom in late summer, the clouds would bring a little squall, mostly wind but occasionally some rain. The clouds she was watching now didn't look very threatening. They would probably blow out to sea long before they reached the Laguna coast.

Annette watched idly as a small sailing boat came into sight far out around the finger of sand dunes and rocks that rimmed the bay to the south. The breeze was filling its single sail and it was moving along at a good clip.

I'd like to be out there in that, she thought lazily. It's funny how some summers almost everybody you know has a boat and then, like this summer, the kids with boats are all vacationing somewhere else.

She had spent part of her vacation at

Moonstone Bay, several hours' drive to the north.

Her visit there had turned into a thrilling adventure as she helped along the romance of her new friend, Sandy Burnett, a lonely young rich girl. But once the excitement was over and everything was going smoothly for Sandy, Annette had been glad to get home to Aunt Lila and Uncle Archie in Hollywood. They were her father's sister and bachelor brother, and they had been like second parents to her since the accident that had orphaned her several years earlier.

After a few days at home, Annette felt ready to spend the rest of her vacation at their Laguna Beach cottage. As usual, she expected to invite several of her crowd to come down and be her houseguests. But to her dismay, she found that practically everyone she really liked in the crowd was out of town. Some were traveling with their families, like Jinks Bradley and his Aunt Tish, the painter. Others, like Lisa Kerry, had gone home to other states for the summer. They were all coming back well before school started, but it would be lonely until then.

When she discovered that Babs Gray was home from a trip around the country with her mother and father and was free to join her at Laguna, Annette had been delighted.

Babs wasn't as close a friend of Annette's as Lisa Kerry had come to be, but she lived just across the street in Hollywood, and she and Annette were in and out of each other's homes all the time. Babs was full of fun and as attractive in her blond way as Annette was in her own dark beauty. She was popular with the crowd, too, though she had none of Annette's talents for singing and dancing and was not in the least athletically inclined.

The Grays, who were very strict with Babs, had been glad to let her go to the beach house with the McCleods and Annette. Aunt Lila and Uncle Archie loved their niece very dearly, but they were never overindulgent. Uncle Archie especially could be quite stern when the occasion called for it.

Annette rested her chin on her knees and

studied the little sloop far out in the choppy bay. It seemed to be changing course now and working its way toward the shore. It was still too far out for her to recognize the two men who were in it, even if she knew them. She decided idly that it probably belonged to one of the summer residents along the bay shore. Some of the older houses were rental properties, leased for summer. They often had several sets of occupants during the season. At any rate, she didn't know anyone who owned a sailboat exactly like that. Whoever the man at the tiller was, though, he knew how to sail. Annette had gotten a lot of sailing experience several years ago when Uncle Archie had his catboat and taught her how to handle it.

The breeze was quickening, and Annette thought she'd heard a tiny sneeze from the direction of Babs's beach mat. She decided it was time to rouse her friend and start her moving about. Babs was one of those people who caught colds easily.

"Hey, there, sleeping beauty!" She leaned

over and shook Babs's shoulder. "Wake up and start thinking about some cute ideas for the welcome-home party Saturday night for Lisa and all the rest of our gang."

Babs sat up with a groan, rubbing her eyes. "You think for both of us. I'm simply exhausted. That second swim around the end of the dock just about finished me. I guess I'll never make the Olympic team after all." She stretched and yawned and was about to lie back and relax again when she caught Annette's stern eye. She moaned and sat up straight. "Oh, all right. But I thought it was already decided that we'd have a Hawaiian whatsit. I've forgotten what Rod Lang called it, but you seemed to think he was a genius for suggesting it."

"The word is luau, loo-*ow*. It means a feast, Rod says. He went to two of them in July when he was on the Islands with his dad and mother. He says they're lots of fun, once you get all the work done that you have to do ahead of time."

"I hope he and Neil Rogers will take time out from their surfboarding and skin diving to help us with that work!" Babs said with a toss of her head. "Boys make me so tired! They're full of ideas about what to do, and then *we* have to do it while they pose and show off their muscles."

"It won't be like that this time. Rod's really excited about making this a big thing. He has all sorts of Hawaiian souvenirs that he and his family brought back from the Islands. His dad says he can borrow them for the party if we take good care of them."

"That sounds terrific!" Babs was beginning to become interested herself. "I know where I can get a real grass skirt to wear. How about you?"

"Oh, Aunt Lila's already starting to whip up a muumuu for me to wear. I think she has one in mind for you, too, in a different color."

"Oh, marvelous!" Babs gave a deep sigh of relief. "To tell the truth, that grass skirt I was boasting about has been hanging in our attic ever since Mom wore it to a Halloween party when I was about seven! I'm afraid if I tried to hula in it, it would break into little pieces like shredded wheat!"

"We can do without *that* bit," Annette said, laughing.

Babs nodded in vigorous agreement; then she grew serious. "It's going to cost quite a bit, isn't it? I mean for the food for everyone and little gag presents for the kids we're welcoming back from vacation."

Annette knitted her brows over the answer. "Well, I suppose if we tried to have a real, authentic luau, it would cost a lot. They cook meat and fish in a pit, Rod says, for hours before the party. And they have all sorts of fruit and vegetables and stuff they call poi that they eat with their fingers and tastes like paperhangers' paste." She ran out of breath and had to start again. "And they have rum and brandy and—but *we* won't. We're having hamburgers and wieners and soda pop, and Rod is going to play his ukulele and we'll have Hawaiian music on the record player while we're sitting around on mats, eating with our fingers." Annette smiled. "We're also going to borrow things like fishnets and shells and colored fishing floats to drape around the front yard. Rod says that Neil knows where he can borrow three or four tiki torches for atmosphere, so we won't need to string lights out from the house."

"And what are tiki torches?" Babs asked.

"Kerosene torches fastened to long poles stuck down in the sand. They're part of the luau."

"I suppose Neil and Rod will *both* bring their ukuleles," Babs said not too enthusiastically.

Annette nodded. "They're working up some kind of an act. Song and dance, I guess. Big secret."

"They can keep their secret. I'll wait and be surprised. I can imagine it will feature Neil. He always shows off so. Rod never does that, I've noticed. He's nicer than Neil, I suppose, but—" Babs hesitated, took her powder compact out of her beach bag, and began slapping powder on her nose.

Annette looked at her sidewise and bit back a smile. Then she finished for Babs, "—but *you* go for the big, handsome football type?"

"Well," Babs began, blushing, "I guess so." Then she added hastily, "Not that he's ever said anything *personal*. He always seems to be thinking about athletics and talking about buying gym stuff to build up his muscles."

"He's probably planning for a career in physical education," Annette guessed. "There's money in that if you're good at it, and heaven knows he's usually moaning about being flat broke. Rod always picks up the check when the four of us get hot dogs at the stand up the beach."

"Well, he probably gets a bigger allowance than Neil," Babs said, defending her hero.

"And Neil spends what *he* gets on himself!" Annette said quietly. "He probably has Rod convinced that he's doing him a favor by letting him pay for treats. It's funny, Neil Rogers and Rod Lang are so different, but they've always seemed to get along just great. I remember when Neil first came to our school in junior high, he would go around talking about how much better everything was back where he used to live. Some of the boys fought with him on account of it but Rod never did."

"Do you mean Rod was afraid of him?" Babs was a bit shocked.

"Goodness, no!" Annette laughed. "He *liked* Neil, and he said Neil had a right to stand up for his old school. It was being loyal, even if what Neil said wasn't always completely true."

"Did the others buy that?" Babs asked idly.

"After a while they got used to Neil, especially when he began sprouting into a star athlete for us. Now most everyone at school thinks he's simply terrific," Annette said.

Babs nodded with a smile. "Including his little self!"

"And how!" Annette agreed quickly.

Babs rubbed suntan lotion on her arms for a moment before she spoke. "I'm going to ask Neil to take me skin-diving next week if the weather's good."

Annette frowned. "You've never been, have you?"

Babs sensed her disapproval. She tossed her

head and laughed. "No, but Neil can show me how. He says he's the best skin diver in that club they have. And he's done a lot of scuba diving. You know, with the rubber suit or whatever it is, and the tank of air. He tells the most exciting stories about the things he's seen underwater."

"Hmm," Annette commented, "like sea serpents, I suppose. Did he slay them with his spear-gun or with his bare hands?" She grinned at Babs's indignant look.

"He didn't mention sea serpents," Babs said with a reproachful pout. "Just sharks and stuff. He's had lots of thrilling fights with them."

"I bet," Annette said with a chuckle.

"Just the same, I'm going to ask him to teach me to skin-dive. You've done some, I know. What's so hard about it?"

Annette shrugged. She didn't want to tell Babs that she wasn't a strong enough swimmer. "I think you should go to a regular teacher. Learn from *him* the right way, and then surprise Neil by knowing how."

As Babs hesitated, still pouting, they heard a

hail. "Ahoy, *wahines*! Ahoy-y!" The shout brought them both to their feet to stare at the small sloop that Annette had watched rounding the point. It was close enough now for them to recognize the occupants. The tall, sandy-haired young man posing beside the single mast was Neil. At the tiller, doing the real work of steering the little sailboat safely up to the dock, was Rod Lang, a slim, dark-haired boy.

"Hi, Neil! Hi, Rod!" Annette shouted, cupping her hands around her mouth. "Where did you steal that?"

Neil's happy smile faded and he scowled at her for a moment, but Babs's squeal of admiration brought back his proud grin. Rod was too busy bringing the sloop in to react to Annette's teasing.

"What was that word Neil called us? *Wah-*something. What does it mean?" Babs asked hastily, taking time to powder her nose again as they waited.

Annette smiled. "Wahine means woman or girl in Hawaiian. Wah-*hee*-nee. Neil was just showing off his vocabulary—which I'll bet Rod taught him not five minutes ago!"

"Wahine," Babs said, pouting. "I thought it meant something sort of—uh—"

"Like 'darling,' huh?" Annette teased, and she saw Babs's cheeks grow pink under the suntan lotion.

"Of course not!" Babs tried to sound indignant, but Annette's dark eyes twinkled at her and she fled quickly toward the dock, with Annette following close behind her.

There was a swagger in Neil's broad shoulders as he tied up the little sailboat and adjusted the rope fenders so the rough side of the old dock would not scratch the paint. "Pretty neat, isn't she?" Neil asked Babs as he leaped gracefully to the dock to greet them.

"It's perfectly darling!" Babs agreed breathlessly. "Is it yours?"

Before Neil could answer, Rod laughed. "No such luck!"

Neil flashed him a frown and said with a touch of annoyance, "It's as good as mine for a

few days. Jim Payson had to go up to the city with his family and he left the critter in my charge. She's a neat little number."

"Oh, yes!" Babs said, wide-eyed. "Sailing must be a big kick. I've only ridden in cruisers, and the engines make such a racket! Really, it must be heavenly to go gliding along without that noise." She smiled up hopefully at the tall young man.

"Yeah, it's a gas, all right," Neil admitted. "We're on our way to do some skin-diving."

"Oh?" Babs's blue eyes lit up. "That should be fun!"

"Yeah," Neil agreed. He turned to Annette. "Hey, do you think your aunt would donate a couple of bottles of soda pop to take along? We forgot to stock up at Jim's place when we picked up the yacht, and skin diving's a thirsty business."

"Why—" Annette hesitated only a second. She wanted to tell Neil he had a lot of gall, but she controlled herself quickly. "Why, I'm sure she'd love to. And if you smile pretty at her, she might even add a slice of her special chocolate cake. I know there's some left over from last night."

"Oh, we couldn't ask for anything to eat," Rod said quickly. "We have nerve enough asking for pop."

Neil scowled at him. "Aw, come on. Stop being so noble." He turned to Annette. "Keep an eye on the tub, will you? We'll be right back." He took Rod's arm and led him up toward the house.

"Just like that!" Annette said with a shrug. "Big deal."

Babs's eyes flashed. "At least he could have offered to take us for a *little* ride." She frowned at Annette. "And you acting sweet as honey to the big oaf."

Annette smiled mysteriously. "I just wanted to get rid of them for a few minutes."

"Why?" Babs demanded crossly.

"Because we're going to play a little joke on them. They didn't invite us to go with them, so we'll just wait till they're out of sight in the house and then take their precious boat and go for a sail ourselves!" Annette's eyes danced with mischief.

"Neat! Where will we go?" Babs was ready.

"Oh, not far," Annette said confidently. "Just inside the bay here. But they won't know that when they see us. They'll think we really mean to sail away. And then we'll turn around and come back and say, 'Thanks for the lovely sail!'"

2

Trouble

The two girls waited until Neil and Rod had gone into the McCleod cottage. Then Annette gave Babs quick orders and they slipped into the little sloop.

In a couple of minutes they had run up the sail and cast off. Annette took her place at the tiller. As a light breeze caught the tall sail, the boat moved out smoothly from the dock. The water was calm inside the bay, but Annette could see that it was kicking up a little beyond the point. The clouds she had seen earlier in the south now seemed bigger and moving north a bit faster. For a moment she considered coming about and running back to the dock.

But as she hesitated, Babs called out from her post amidships, "Isn't this super? I knew I'd love sailing!"

Annette decided that they might as well have a few minutes more of it before they went in. "Oh, yes, it's quite a kick!" she agreed.

A small wave struck the bow and sprinkled Babs. She laughed at the shower and hung onto the mainsheet as the sail bellied out and the small boat took on speed. The wind had come. It wasn't a steady wind. It came in little gusts and made steering difficult. More and more water splashed over the sides.

Wish I'd turned back when I should have, Annette thought. And suddenly she remembered something. They hadn't put on life jackets. Of all the rules of safety that Uncle Archie had drummed into her head while they sailed the cat-boat, the most urgent one was "Always wear a life jacket when you're sailing a small boat." She had forgotten it completely until now.

Babs was watching the shore for the boys to come out on the dock and miss their boat. "No sign yet," she reported with a giggle.

"Well, we'd better go back now, anyhow. They'll be there when we get in." Annette kept her voice calm as she added, "By the way, hand me that line and you go forward to the locker and get out the life jackets. The boys will razz us if they see we're not wearing them."

"Life jackets? Oh, Annette! Girls look so silly in those things! Why do we care what those characters think of us?" Babs pouted.

Annette frowned. There was a sharpness in her voice that she couldn't avoid as she answered Babs. "Don't argue, Babs. It's a safety rule. Everybody does it. You don't want them to think we're dopes who don't know the rules, do you?"

Babs reacted hastily. "Okay, okay!" She crawled aft, handed over the mainsheet, and then started forward to the locker.

Annette could feel a stronger pull on the rudder now. The smoothness of the bay had turned into choppy little waves, and the wind was starting to come in stronger gusts. "Careful—keep to the high side, Babs!" she called as Babs ducked to one side to avoid a splatter and tipped the little boat dangerously.

Annette turned to look shoreward. She could

see the two young men now, running down toward the dock. Neil was waving his arms wildly. Now he stopped to cup his mouth and yell out toward the sailboat, but the wind took his words away.

I'm glad I don't have to hear what he thinks of us right now! Annette thought a little grimly. Then she called out, "Hi, Babs! What's the matter?"

Babs was searching the locker. She turned around, letting the lid fall. "No life jackets here. I guess our big strong boyfriends decided they wouldn't pay attention to the rules, either." She laughed, but the laugh broke off suddenly as she saw Annette's sober expression. "Why do you look like that? We're turning around to go back right now anyhow, aren't we? Why do we need those silly jackets?" She crawled aft.

Annette decided not to answer. "Here!" she said quickly, thrusting the mainsheet into Babs's hand. "Hang on and do exactly what I tell you. Turning is tricky, so for goodness' sake, keep down so the boom doesn't hit you when it swings!" A gust of wind, a little stronger than any before it, hit the stern of the sailboat as she spoke, and Annette had to fight the rudder to keep the bow from swinging and putting them into the trough of the waves. The sail fluttered and almost lost the wind, but after a moment of near panic Annette had the sloop under control again. But they were not moving shoreward. They were headed north by west. At the rate the wind was blowing them along, they would be past North Point within a couple of minutes and out of sight of the Laguna beach.

"Wh-where are we going now?" Babs's teeth chattered. She was drenched and chilled. "Why don't we just turn around and go back to the dock? I don't want to go out any farther."

"The wind won't let us turn right now," Annette called out cheerfully. "There's a quiet little bay just around the point. We'll head in there and drop anchor till the boys can swim around to us."

Babs looked unhappily at the fast-receding shore. The two young men were running along the beach now at the edge of the water, watching the little sailboat. "Neil is going to be furious with us," she said glumly.

Annette took a quick look back at the shore and waved. She was not at all surprised when Neil answered her wave with a shake of his fist and then resumed running after Rod toward the stretch of rocks and sand that rimmed the bay and stretched out to the jutting promontory of North Point. She tried to remember from her sailing days with Uncle Archie what the next bay was like. She hoped desperately that they would find shelter just around the edge of the rocky point. Once out of the full force of the wind, she could guide the small sloop to a safe anchorage in calm water.

But this proved impossible. By the time they had reached North Point, Annette had to tack sharply to avoid running aground on half-submerged rocks, and this maneuver took the sloop farther out to sea. Pitching and tossing, they were carried past the entrance to the bay.

Neil and Rod, breathlessly climbing the rocks, almost exhausted from their long run, came to the point just in time to see the tiny sailboat disappearing around another arm of land.

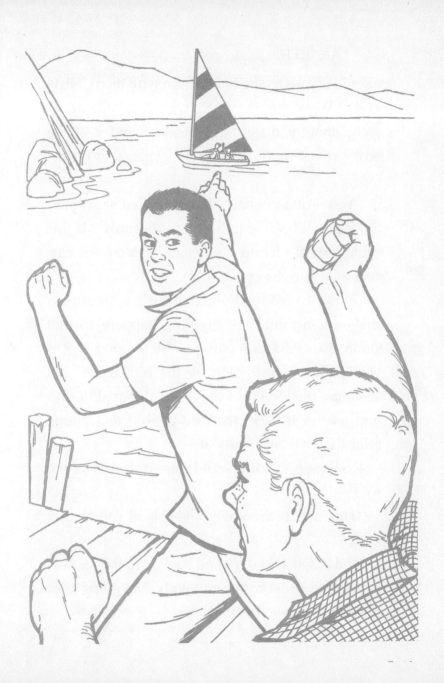

"It's no use trying to catch up with them," Rod said. "We'll just have to wait for Annette to come about and sail back. And I wonder—" He broke off abruptly, a worried expression on his face.

"You wonder what?" Neil growled angrily.

"If she'll be able to," Rod said grimly. "If this squall doesn't let up soon, she's liable to be carried miles up the coast."

"What can we do about it? It's a fine mess she's got me into! If anything happens to that sloop, Jim Payson's going to blame *me*! It was *your* bright idea to stop by the McCleods' and show the boat to those two. And all our skin-diving gear in it!" He scowled at Rod and glared after the vanished sailboat.

Rod turned abruptly and started back over the rocks.

"Hey, where are you going?" Neil yelled after him.

Rod stopped and looked back. "To beg or borrow a motorboat from somebody. I'm going after those kids."

"A motorboat in this kind of sea? You're out of your mind!" Neil barked.

Rod wheeled and started off again. Neil hesitated a moment and then strode after him, grumbling.

"I guess we ought to go after them, at that," Neil admitted as they hurried back toward the beach. Then he stopped suddenly. "Hey, look. There's a neat little single-cabin cruiser parked at the dock at the old Garrett place."

"And a couple of guys going aboard! Let's see if we can flag them down and talk them into taking us to catch up with the girls!" Rod said excitedly, breaking into a run.

Neil was close on his heels at once.

But long before they were within hailing distance of the Garrett dock, the shiny small cruiser had pulled away from the dock and was headed out toward the open sea with one man at the wheel and the other sitting in the cockpit. Although they must have heard the boys yelling, there was no sign from either man that they had noticed it. They didn't even look back.

"Probably thought we were a couple of beach bums looking for a free ride." Neil growled.

Rod's eyes scanned the beach. Not one dock along the row of private beaches had a boat beside it. "I guess we'd better hotfoot it up to the McCleods' and tell Aunt Lila what's going on. She might know somebody with a motorboat they're not using." They started on the run.

"Hey, look! The clouds are getting thinner. Looks like the wind's dying down," Neil said, panting as they ran.

"I sure hope so!" Rod said fervently. "If it does, Annette and Babs can easily slide into one of the little bays between here and Smugglers' Cove." But he added grimly to himself, "Unless they've already been blown too far out to sea!"

But they hadn't been. As a matter of fact, once Annette had decided that the safest course was to run before the wind till the squall was over, the little sloop had been behaving nobly.

They passed several small bays, but Annette noticed that they were not sheltered from the wind. Even if they managed to change course and enter one of those coves, they might find themselves just as badly off as before.

"How much farther do we have to go before we can land somewhere?" Babs asked with chattering teeth. She was huddled down as far as possible, but it was still not enough to shield her from the wind and salt spray.

"Not far," Annette answered as cheerfully as she could. "The wind's dying down. Can't you notice it?"

"No," Babs answered tearfully. "I think you're just making it up."

"No, honestly, Babs! It's slackening. Look at the sail. It's flopping a little."

Babs brightened as she saw that Annette was telling the truth. "Thank goodness!" she cried.

"Babs! I think I know where we are. See that headland sticking out right ahead? The cliff, I mean. I recognize it! Uncle Archie used to come here to fish for sea bass, when he had his boat. I came with him a couple of times to watch." Annette's voice was excited now.

"So?" Babs asked doubtfully.

"There's a cove just around the corner where we dropped anchor to have our lunch. It's sheltered from the wind just like our own bay at Laguna. Once we get past the cliff, we'll head in there!"

"Well, thank goodness!" Babs felt so much better that she laughed. "Just let me know what to do to help."

"Don't worry, I will! We'll have to go on a starboard tack and—" she broke off as the sound of a motorboat engine came faintly from behind them. "I hear a motorboat!"

Babs sat up straight and looked past Annette's shoulder. "It *is* one. It's coming right after us! It must be the boys! They've borrowed a speedboat!"

Annette kept her grip on the tiller while she turned her head for a quick glance. The motorboat was still a long way behind them, and the rough water between the two boats made it impossible to see who was at the wheel. But she was sure it had to be either Neil or Rod. She felt like bursting into tears of relief.

3
Smugglers' Cove

The speedy cruiser was still a considerable distance behind the girls in the small sailboat as Annette maneuvered past the high headland and around into the shelter of Smugglers' Cove.

The water was not completely smooth, but it was a great deal calmer than it had been in the seaway. Now the wind was blowing in gentle gusts that kept the sail filled and made steering easy. Overhead, most of the scurrying clouds were disappearing to the north as the storm moved past.

The two girls looked at each other. "What a relief!" Babs shuddered. "I was never so wet in my life!"

Annette took one hand off the tiller for the first time in what seemed like hours. Her hands were so tired from gripping the wooden bar that she could hardly move her stiff fingers.

"Ouch!" she cried with a wry expression. "I'm glad I don't have to play a violin right now!"

Babs blinked startled eyes at her and then giggled a bit hysterically. "Oh, Annette! I thought for sure we were going to be drowned, and you can joke about it!"

Annette sobered at once. "I don't really think it's funny, Babs. I was as scared as you were. I'm just trying to pull myself together so I can stand hearing what Neil and Rod think about my stupid idea of playing a trick on them that might have ended in a mess."

"I went along with it, so they can blame me, too," Babs told her stoutly. "And if they try to be too mean—" She broke off at the sudden sound of the motorboat engine and looked back toward the point of land. "—Well, here they come now! Get ready for the bawling out!"

Annette let the sail flutter down. "We'll wait for them like little lambs," she told Babs as the sailboat's bow dipped and rose gently.

But Babs had gotten a good look at the two

men in the cruiser that was coming toward them. "Annette! It isn't Neil and Rod at all! It's two perfectly strange men!"

Annette took a quick look and saw that Babs was right. She had never seen either of the men before. At least, not that she remembered. The one at the wheel was a big fellow in a bright orange sweater. She got only a brief look at the man seated in the cockpit, but her impression was that he was wearing more formal clothes and had a yachting cap perched at a jaunty angle on the side of his head. He was watching them through a pair of binoculars which covered part of his face, but what she saw of it was not familiar.

"Must be one of the summer renters that the boys have talked into coming after us," she called to Babs, and she smiled and waved.

Babs scrambled to her feet by hanging onto the mast and called out a friendly "Hi!" to the approaching boat.

But the small cruiser suddenly veered off when it was less than a hundred feet away and, without a sign from either of the men, made a fast circle around the sloop. The powerful engines kicked up a wake that made the choppy bay waters boil and sent a big wave rolling toward the sailboat.

There was no chance to avoid it. The sailboat was due for a bouncing. Annette was angry and dismayed as she watched the cruiser roar off without standing by to see the result of its helmsman's careless disregard for their safety.

"Hang on, Babs!" she shouted, bracing herself at the tiller as she tried desperately to keep the sailboat's bow headed into the approaching wave.

But Babs had been so surprised by the strangers' rude maneuver that she ignored the warning and continued to glare indignantly after the disappearing motorboat. "Of all the poisonous tricks—" she exclaimed angrily, but she had no time to finish. In spite of Annette's efforts, the oncoming wave struck the small craft broadside and rocked it violently. Babs's grip on the mast was wrenched loose, and over she went to disappear into the churning sea.

There was no use trying to control the tossing boat. When Babs failed to come to the surface after a moment, Annette wasted no time. She dived in after her.

It was a good thing that she had. Babs, terrified, was floundering blindly. Annette got a good grip on her and shot to the surface.

"You're all right now," she told Babs firmly. "Take it easy and we'll be back in the boat in a minute."

But it wasn't to be that simple. The abandoned sloop was over on its side, its mast lying flat on the water in a tangle of ropes, its hull half submerged. Floating nearby were the fins and goggles of the boys' skin-diving equipment, already rapidly sinking from sight.

Annette drew Babs toward the bottom of the hull and guided her to a firm grip on the sturdy centerboard. "We'll hang on here for a few minutes till we catch our breath," she told her calmly.

Babs clutched it and hung on desperately, but her panic was passing now that she saw that

Annette was calm. "Those two! If they're friends of Neil's, I don't think much of his taste!"

Annette didn't, either. "I suppose it was their idea of a joke to get even with us for taking the boat. I expect them back any minute, and I bet their faces will be red when they see what their little stunt did!"

"They might have drowned us!" Babs cried.

"They probably didn't think it out that far. It seemed funny to bounce us around and give us a scare, I guess. The morons!"

"I hope they come back soon," Babs said, her teeth chattering. "The water's getting awfully cold."

Annette raised herself out of the water to listen. But there was no sound of the cruiser's engines. As she turned to say something cheerful, she saw that Babs was shaking and shivering. Annette was worried now.

She turned and looked shoreward. The beach was rimmed with big rocks, but there was a stretch of clear sand at the foot of the canyon that led up into the hills overlooking the cove. The tops of some tall palm trees were visible back in the canyon. Annette remembered her uncle's saying that no one lived in the canyon now, but that the bay had acquired its name of Smugglers' Cove when rumrunners had kept a shack there during the Prohibition Era many years earlier. The palm trees had been a landmark.

With the water calming rapidly, it shouldn't be too hard to swim to shore if the cruiser didn't return, Annette thought. She wondered how long she ought to wait. Babs was getting weaker, Annette could tell. Her lips were blue under the lipstick.

Maybe those two were just a couple of clowns trying to act smart, and they're miles away by now, Annette thought suddenly. "We're going to have to swim for it," she told Babs. "We'd better not wait any longer."

Babs was willing. Anything Annette wanted to do was all right with her.

"Maybe I'll warm up swimming," she said hopefully.

"It's not far," Annette told her. "Let's go!"

They pushed off from the hull and swam side by side for several minutes. Then Babs began to drop back, though she tried hard to keep up with Annette.

"Atta girl," Annette encouraged her, dropping back beside her. "Keep it up!"

"I'm afraid I can't make it," Babs said, gasping.

"Sure you can! Turn over and float now. I'll do the lifeguard rescue bit. Just kick a little and off we go!" Annette told her confidently.

Babs rolled over and Annette took her in tow. "When I'm rested, I'll tow you," Babs said as they started out.

But Annette, though she agreed cheerfully, knew that Babs was very close to exhaustion. There was no likelihood that she could do any more swimming today. If they were to reach shore, Annette would have to do it all.

And do it she did, though she thought several times before reaching the beach that she might not make it.

When they finally were safe on the sandy

beach, they staggered up to a dry stretch and gratefully collapsed in the hot sunshine.

In a very few minutes they were both sound asleep, so sound asleep that neither stirred when the sailboat washed ashore on the crest of the rising tide and lodged between two piles of sharp rocks, snapping the mast in two and cracking several planks in the hull.

Nor did either of them awaken half an hour later when a gray-bearded man in an artist's smock and beret came down to the shore out of the canyon and stopped in surprise at the sight of the wrecked sloop and the two girls asleep not far from it. For a minute he stared at them, pulling at his beard and scowling. Then he took a large brassbound telescope out of its case and leveled it at the horizon. There was nothing to see but open water. He lowered the telescope and listened, cupping his ear toward the water. But there was nothing to be heard except the pounding of the surf.

After a moment, scowling toward the sleeping girls, he put away the telescope and strode out of sight into the canyon.

The sun was still high when Annette sat up and looked around her in slight bewilderment. The sight of Babs still sleeping beside her reminded her of what had happened. She looked quickly for the wrecked sloop, but there was no sign of it on the smooth surface of the water. She groaned unhappily at the thought that it was probably at the bottom of the cove. She wasn't sure just how much sailboats like that cost, but she knew that whatever it was, she was responsible for its loss. And that paying for it was going to be a big problem in her life.

Uncle Archie and Aunt Lila gave her a generous allowance for clothes and school expenses, and she had a small savings account. But even by the wildest stretch of imagination, she couldn't see how she could pay for the boat, get the clothing she needed for school, and pay her share of the luau expenses!

Babs's voice interrupted her thoughts. "I feel lots better, don't you?" Babs was sitting up.

"Some ways," Annette answered glumly. "I was just trying to figure how much my silly joke was going to cost, now that the boat is sunk!"

"But it isn't sunk," Babs said. "It's right over between those mean-looking rocks." She pointed.

Annette was on her feet in a flash. Sure enough, the bow of the sloop was poking out between the rocks. "Thank goodness for that! No matter what damage has been done, it can't be as bad as sinking the whole boat!"

"No sign of the boys," Babs said, staring out to sea. "Oh, Annette! Suppose we have to stay here all night!"

"We can always climb up and try to find a road," Annette told her soothingly, turning her gaze toward the canyon and the hills beyond. "There's bound to be *some* kind of road." She tried to be cheerful. Then, suddenly: "Hey! Maybe somebody does live back there, after all! See that line of telephone poles coming down the hill into the canyon? That means there's a phone!"

"What are we waiting for?" Babs demanded excitedly. "Let's go."

4

The Threat

There *was* a house in the canyon. It was a tiny place with a garden and a brilliant scarlet bougainvillea vine climbing to the roof. Nearby, a small red barn added a picturesque touch.

The two girls stopped and took in the scene. "It can't be real," Babs said, wide-eyed. "It's a postcard."

Annette laughed. "It should be. An artist lives there. See that north window in the barn? That's a sure sign."

"Why?" Babs was surprised.

"The light in the studio doesn't keep changing when you have a window facing north, because the sun doesn't ever come from that direction."

"Oh, I see!" Babs nodded. "I can imagine how confusing it would be if you started painting when the sun was shining in and everything looked bright and pretty. Then when you went for lunch and came back, the sun wasn't coming in anymore and everything looked different."

"Right," Annette agreed. Then she looked woebegone. "Lunch! We never had any. What are we standing here gabbing for when there may be a perfectly charming artist in that house just dying to give us some hot tea and English muffins with marmalade!"

"You're killing me!" Babs laughed, but she was at least two steps ahead of Annette as they hurried toward the cottage.

When they were still some distance from the front door, a small boy with dark eyes and jet-black hair let himself down out of the branches of an ancient oak tree beside the path and darted toward the house.

"Little boy! Is anybody home?" Annette called after him.

But he didn't stop until he was at the door, his hand on the doorknob. Then he turned to look back at them, and even at a distance they could see that he seemed to be frightened. A moment later, he had darted into the house and had slammed the door behind him.

The two girls hesitated uncertainly. "I suppose he's telling his mother that two lost mermaids came after him! He looked as if he thought we were going to eat him up!" Babs complained. "What now?"

Annette laughed. "We'll knock politely. I'm sure his mommy must know that mermaids only eat fish." She linked her arm into Babs's and they went on together. "Just smile your prettiest when she opens the door."

But the woman who opened the door at their knock and stared hard at them didn't look as if their smiles would win them an invitation to tea. "What do you wish? Who sent you to this house?" she demanded. Her voice was soft in spite of her words, and her accent sounded as if she spoke Spanish. Her dark-complexioned face was stern under a halo of heavy gray braids.

Annette was startled to see that the woman was holding a heavy poker at her side. It was only partly concealed by her skirt. "We were shipwrecked back there in the cove, and we'd like to use your telephone if we may, please."

The woman still eyed her suspiciously. "There is no telephone. It was taken away before we came to this place to live."

"Oh, no!" Babs groaned. "No phone! It isn't possible!"

Even Annette looked crushed by the news. "Okay, thanks anyhow. I guess we'll start walking back to town."

But the woman flashed a sudden smile and told them, "I am sorry for the telephone, señoritas, but, you see, my husband is an artist. He likes the quiet for his work. But it is a pity you must walk."

"Oh, I guess we can stand it. It can't be more than a few miles," Annette told her cheerfully. "Come on, Babs." She started to turn away.

But Babs had ideas of her own. "All right, but don't be surprised if I faint or something. I feel awfully dizzy." She held her hand over her eyes and swayed.

"*¡Ay, pobrecitas!*" The woman held out her

hand to them. "Do not hurry away. You must rest and be refreshed. I will make you some chocolate and you shall have some of my *bizcochitos*!" She flung open the door, drew them inside, and offered the cookies.

A rear door closed noisily as they entered with their hostess. Annette guessed that the little boy had fled that way. Evidently, he was not as ready to accept them as the woman was.

"Oh, what perfectly stunning paintings!" Babs stood in the middle of the sunny living room and gazed at the group of vivid, modern pictures on the walls.

The woman smiled proudly. "They are all the work of my husband. But, of course, you have already recognized the technique of Francisco Marino." She waited expectantly.

Babs looked blank, but Annette spoke quickly with a smile. "I'm afraid we're awfully ignorant about modern paintings, Señora Marino, but we think it's fascinating. And the colors are gorgeous."

"Ah, well," Señora Marino smiled warmly,

"there is plenty of time to learn. Even the artists do not agree! And now, please be at home while I make a little refreshment for you and my small grandson. I will not be gone long."

She waved them to two handsome mahogany chairs before the crackling fire and then whisked out of the room into the kitchen. A moment later they heard her calling, "Pablo! Pablo! *¡Adelante! * Friends are here."

"Golly!" Babs looked at a great carved chest in a corner. "You'd never guess what lovely things they have from the size of the house! I didn't know painters were ever rich enough to have furniture and stuff like this!"

"I wonder what country they're from?" Annette whispered.

"Could be Spain, I guess, or a South American country," Babs answered under her breath. "Look at that portrait on the little inlaid table, the man in the uniform with all the medals. I bet he's somebody big. I think I'll ask her."

"I don't think it would be polite," Annette kept her voice down, "but if we keep looking at it every now and then, Señora Marino might tell us without being asked."

They tried this when the pot of steaming, foamy chocolate with its scent of cinnamon was brought in, but Señora Marino failed to take the hint.

And there was no sign of the boy, Pablo.

They were both finishing their second cup of chocolate and nibbling their fifth or sixth crisp cookie when Annette noticed that Señora Marino glanced uneasily from time to time toward the open door. She was trying to seem interested in Babs's account of their adventure in the sailboat, but it was all too evident to Annette that her mind was on something else. Annette guessed that it might be the absent child. She decided it was time they left. He was probably still frightened of them.

She signaled to Babs and got up. "I think we'd better start for home. It's a very long walk," she reminded Babs briskly.

She couldn't help noticing that Señora Marino made no protest at their going, and even though she insisted on their taking along some *bizcochitos* to nibble on during the long walk homeward, she seemed almost glad they were going. She walked to the door with them to point out the path that would take them to the top of the hill where a road ran parallel to the ocean. It was old and bumpy, but eventually it led into a paved road that in a mile or so crossed the highway to Laguna.

"It is too bad we have no automobile," she told the girls, "or my husband would gladly take you to your home."

"Oh, we wouldn't have thought of interrupting his painting, anyhow," Annette assured her. "Besides, we don't mind walking—very much."

But as they said good-bye and started up the hill, she was not so sure that Señor Marino would have been as obliging about chauffeuring them as his wife seemed to think. They saw Pablo standing in the doorway of the red studio barn with a stocky, gray-bearded man in an artist's smock and beret. The man had his arm draped protectively over the little boy's shoulders, and both were scowling blackly at the girls.

When they reached the top of the hill, the girls turned and looked back. On an impulse Annette waved to the man and boy, who were still watching. There was no answering wave. Instead, the man turned his back abruptly and led the little boy into the barn. The door slammed so hard that they could hear the sound even up on the hill.

"Well, after all"—Annette laughed as they went on—"we ate a lot of his cookies and drank his chocolate, so naturally he's glad to see us go!"

"I don't know what it is about us today," Babs said, half seriously, "but we certainly don't seem a bit popular with the men we've met so far!"

Annette snorted. "And when the boys find out what happened to Jim Payson's precious boat, we're going to be poison with a capital *P*!"

They trudged on in thoughtful silence for a few minutes. It wasn't easy going. Their beach shoes had gone overboard with the skin-diving gear, and they were finding the road a bit rough for their bare feet.

Annette stopped suddenly, gripping Babs's arm. "Listen!" she said eagerly. "What's that?"

Babs gave a little shriek. "A snake?"

"No, silly! That noise. A motor. There, look up there!"

She pointed to the big helicopter flying a few hundred feet above the sea. "Coast Guard! Probably looking for us!"

They waved their arms wildly to signal to it, but the copter stayed on course toward the north. "Oh, they didn't see us!" Babs was tired and discouraged. She sat down on the nearest rock and sneezed a couple of times. "I guess we're stuck with walking," she said plaintively.

Annette had been watching the helicopter. It had circled suddenly out of sight in the general direction of Smugglers' Cove. "They've spotted the sloop, I imagine," she told Babs excitedly. "They'll land and look for us, and the Marinos will tell them we're walking home."

And that is exactly what did happen. It was hardly ten minutes before the two girls, waiting expectantly, watched the helicopter climb into sight and start in their direction. A moment later it was hovering overhead and making a landing.

Rod and Neil were hurrying toward the girls before the rotor blades had stopped whirling.

"Are you two all right?" Rod got to them first.

"We are now," Annette said. "Are we ever glad to see you and that whirlybird! Our feet were giving out."

Neil strode up, his blond hair windblown and his face covered with a scowl. "Whose goofy idea was it to steal our boat and wreck it?" he barked.

"Nobody's!" Annette's dark eyes flashed. "As it happens, the only idea I had was to borrow the thing for a few minutes because you didn't have the courtesy to invite us for a ride."

Neil's face reddened. "I didn't think about it till we were in the house talking to your aunt, and when we came out, you and the boat were gone."

"That's right, Annette," Rod said. "We did talk about taking you kids for a short sail."

"Well, anyhow, I'm sorry now I ever took the boat," Annette admitted sadly. "I'll pay for any damages."

"But it wasn't our fault the silly boat was wrecked!" Babs said indignantly between sniffles. "It was those two characters in the cruiser. They should pay!"

"How did it happen, Annette?" Rod asked. "What characters is she talking about?"

Annette explained hastily. "— And they just dashed away without stopping to see if they'd caused any trouble!" she concluded.

"What was the registry number on the bow of the cruiser?" Rod asked eagerly. "We'll hunt them up."

Annette shrugged expressively. "We had no time to notice."

"Oh!" Rod looked grim. "Well, that's that, then. There are hundreds of little single-cabin jobs like that dashing around here. Not much chance you'll be able to find out who they were."

"I suppose you're right," Annette said sadly. The pilot of the helicopter was signaling them to come. He had the motors going. "All aboard, folks! You're using up Uncle Sam's gasoline with that coffee klatch! Let's travel!"

They piled in silently, and it was only after they were airborne that Annette broke the gloomy silence to ask, "Did you have a look at the boat? Is there a lot of damage? What do you think it will cost me?"

"We can get a secondhand mast at the ship chandler's, and if we do the repairs ourselves, the whole thing won't run over a hundred dollars," Neil told her.

"Oh!" It was an unhappy sigh. "I guess I'll have to ask Uncle Archie to help me out."

"The thing is to get started tomorrow morning," Rod said gravely, "after what the old guy at the cove had to say."

"Señor Marino? Did you talk to him?" Annette asked, surprised.

"Not much," Rod told her with a grimace. "*He* did the talking. We listened. He says the cove is his private property, and if we don't have our boat out of there in twenty-four hours, he'll have it towed out to sea and sunk!"

5

Salvage Operations

"Can he do that legally?" Annette asked, shocked.

Rod looked worried and Neil scowled. "We can't wait to find out. We may have to step the mast in later and wait to repaint, but if we can get the planks replaced tomorrow, we can row the sloop out of the cove by Marino's deadline."

"I'll talk to Uncle Archie right away about the repairs," Annette promised gloomily. "I'm sure he'll lend me the money and let me pay it back out of my allowance." But she added, "I hope!" silently.

"Wish we didn't have to take it from you," Rod said.

Annette tried to smile reassuringly. "Don't worry about it. Uncle Archie's always very understanding."

"I sure hope so," Neil said, frowning.

The big helicopter landed in the alley behind the McCleod beach house. Aunt Lila and Uncle Archie had been waiting anxiously for it, and they ran to greet the girls as the pilot let the copter down and idled the engine.

Aunt Lila was almost tearful with relief as she hugged both tired girls, and when Uncle Archie tried to look stern and started to scold Annette, she whisked them away to the house.

"I'll talk to you later, young woman," her uncle called after Annette, and he went to shake hands with the pilot before the copter took off again for the heliport. "And now, young fellows," he turned back to the two boys standing by uncertainly, "suppose you bring me up-to-date on my niece's activities this afternoon."

It was quite a bit later when Annette saw her uncle again. Babs had been ordered to bed at once by Aunt Lila, who had also prescribed hot lemonade with honey for their houseguest.

Annette drank some of the lemonade, too, to please Aunt Lila. But it hadn't tasted as good as

usual. She was too worried about how to break the news to Uncle Archie that she needed to borrow money from him.

When she did get up the courage to approach Uncle Archie in his study, she heard him talking to someone. The other voice was that of a man with a foreign accent. It was a soft, pleasant voice and laugh, and its owner was apparently enjoying his visit.

I suppose he'll be here for dinner, whoever he is, Annette thought disappointedly. Well, I'll just have to catch Uncle Archie after the man's gone. And she went up to Babs's room again.

"What did he say?" Babs bounced up in bed. She was feeling better already from all the care Aunt Lila was giving her. Empty dishes on a supper tray were mute evidence of it.

"Didn't even get a chance to talk to him," Annette admitted, sitting down by the window and looking out past the dock toward the setting sun. "He had company. Some man with the nicest speaking voice. I'm dying to see what he's like. He'll probably stay for dinner."

"Oh, Annette! That's not fair! I'm going to get up and get dressed, too. I want to see him. He may be somebody in TV or the *movies*!"

Annette laughed. "You'd better stay where you are or Aunt Lila will lecture you for spreading germs around!"

Babs groaned and collapsed on her pillows. "Why do I always have to be the one who catches cold?" she asked plaintively.

Annette peered out from behind the sheer curtains with sudden interest. "Oh, oh! He isn't staying for dinner, after all. Uncle Archie's walking him out right now."

Babs shot out of bed and ran to the window. "Where? What's he look like?" she demanded, looking over Annette's shoulder.

"He's sort of old," Annette said gravely. "At least thirty, I'd say." She was disappointed.

Babs clasped her hands. "But so handsome and romantic! I'm sure I've seen a picture of him somewhere! Do you suppose he's a foreign actor?"

"Well, he has an accent, from the few words I

heard him saying to Uncle Archie, so he *could* be someone like that."

"Well, wherever he's from, he certainly is Mister Gorgeous!" Babs giggled.

"Hmph!" Annette took her by the arm. "If you don't get straight back into bed, your cold is going to get worse and you'll miss the luau!"

Down at the gate Uncle Archie parted from his visitor, and the man walked briskly up the strand out of her range. She watched Uncle Archie come indoors and then she moved reluctantly toward the door.

"Wish me luck," she told Babs. "Here I go!" But Uncle Archie had a surprise for her. He had heard the full details of the sailboat's disaster from Neil and Rod, and he had arranged to pay for the repairs they planned to make. "But don't think you are getting off so easily for your childish actions," he told her sternly. "I shall expect to deduct a fair amount from your weekly allowance until I am fully repaid. Perhaps the experience will teach you something."

"I'm sure it will, Uncle Archie," Annette admitted at once.

"Of course," he looked over the top of his glasses at his niece, "with your school term about to start and also this welcome party you've been planning, perhaps we can wait a few weeks before starting the deductions. But not long, you understand. You must learn responsibility."

"Oh, Uncle Archie! You're a perfect lamb, and *so* understanding! I was planning to call all the kids and tell them that there wouldn't be any luau!" She gave her uncle a big hug and dashed off to break the good news to Aunt Lila.

It wasn't much of a surprise to her aunt, since she had already discussed the matter thoroughly with Uncle Archie and had helped him make his decision.

"Now Babs and I can spend all day tomorrow making tissue-paper leis for everyone to wear Saturday night," Annette planned happily. "And the next day, we'll shop—"

But Aunt Lila shook her head and smiled. "I'm afraid you're going to be too busy driving

the boys around to buy the lumber and nails and whatever they need. Your uncle insists that is the least you can do to help undo the damage."

"Oh, okay," Annette agreed. "I guess Uncle Archie's right, but there's so much to do for the party."

"There'll still be time," Aunt Lila said firmly, and Annette knew the matter was settled.

Annette started to go back upstairs to report to Babs. At the door she stopped suddenly. "By the way, Aunt Lila, who was the 'tall, dark, and handsome' that just visited Uncle Archie? We saw him from the window, and Babs is sure he's a movie star at least."

"Babs is wrong. That's our new neighbor at the Garrett place. A very charming young man from somewhere called San Marcos. It's one of those tiny republics in Central America."

"Wasn't there some kind of trouble down there a year or so ago?" Annette knitted her brows.

"I'm sure I don't know, dear," Aunt Lila said. "But I'm certain if there was, Mr. Horton had

nothing to do with it. He's a charming young man and so polite."

"Horton? That's a strange name for a person from Central America." Annette frowned. "Most of them have Spanish last names."

"Oh, it's not the name he uses in his own country. His Spanish name is so hard for people here to pronounce that he uses his English grandfather's name instead."

"How did Uncle Archie meet him? They seem very friendly."

Aunt Lila laughed and held up her hands. "They met in the hardware store yesterday while buying fishing tackle, and they found out they had some of the same ideas about game fishing. That did it. Mr. Horton simply had to come to see your uncle's collection of photographs and trophies."

Annette couldn't restrain a twinkle as she said solemnly, "I've always heard how polite Latin Americans are!"

Aunt Lila twinkled back at her. "Shoo! Run along and break the sad news to Babs that Mr.

Horton is merely a sportsman and not a glamorous movie star. And find out what she'd like for a snack!"

But Babs wasn't entirely discouraged. She still thought Mr. Horton could be a movie star as well as a sportsman. When Annette left early the next morning to drive the boys around in her sports car to do their shopping for lumber and nails and a mast, Babs was comfortably settled in bed, surrounded by piles of fan magazines and fashion monthlies. She was hopeful she would find a picture of the handsome Mr. Horton.

Neil was rather grumpy and made several unkind remarks about the girls having lost the skin-diving equipment from the wrecked sloop. He mentioned it one time too many for Rod, who could see how unhappy Neil's attitude was making Annette.

"Hey, knock it off, will you?" Rod snapped. "Nobody set out to lose that stuff. Besides, we can borrow some masks and fins from one of the other guys and come back and dive for ours, once we have the boat safely out of the cove."

"Yeah, so we can!" Neil agreed, and he was cheerful after that.

The sloop was still wedged between the rocks of Smugglers' Cove when they trooped down from the hillside where Annette parked her car, the Monster. They were all heavily loaded with lumber, tools, and lunch.

It took much lifting, pushing, and grunting, but the boys finally had the wounded sloop high and dry on the sand. They were soon busy with sawing and hammering, and Annette made a point of helping out, too.

Finally, after Neil had barked at her a couple of times for no reason at all, she went back up to the car and brought down her ukulele.

"Good gal!" Rod called cheerfully between hammer blows on the hull. "How about some close harmony on 'Aloha Oe'? I'm a little rusty."

Annette struck a few soft chords of the Hawaiian song of farewell and began to sing. Before she had reached the end of the chorus, both boys had put aside their tools and joined their voices with hers.

None of them noticed the small boy who had come timidly down out of the canyon and was hiding now behind a boulder, listening wide-eyed to their singing. It was little Pablo.

They finished with a bit of harmony that made Rod exclaim, "Hey! We're good!"

"Of course we are!" Annette told him with a lofty wave of her hand. "That's one number that's foolproof." Then she struck a few lively chords and sang to Rod, "Oh, there was a young beachboy—" She broke off, smiling. "Come on, Rod! You've simply got to do that one on Saturday night!"

"Aw, the gang's seen me do it a dozen times!" Rod protested modestly. But Neil dragged him to his feet and over to a patch of soft sand.

"Hit it, Annette!" Neil called, and as she twanged the uke, Rod started his comic dance and song.

It was a comedy hula number about a beach-boy who had always been too lazy to learn to hula. All day he posed languidly for tourist cameras. Then one day as he sat watching a hula contest on the beach, a big crab crept up and fastened its claws to his back. The hula that he did while trying to shake off the attacker won him first prize in the contest, and as it turned out, he had the crab for supper.

Rod's leaps and twists and funny faces so amused Pablo that the child started laughing and came out of hiding. He clapped his hands in applause at the end; then he suddenly became aware that the three strangers were watching him. He stood frozen, staring, for a moment, and then as Annette laid aside her uke and called, "Pablo! Come here!" he turned and fled up toward the canyon.

"Who on earth—?" Neil exclaimed with a scowl.

"The little boy I told you about—the Marinos' grandson," she explained hastily, and hurried after Pablo.

She overtook the boy as he started to climb into his favorite tree near the cottage. "Please, Pablo. Don't be afraid. We are friends."

"I know you came to eat *bizcochitos* and

chocolate with *mi abuela* yesterday, but the others—" He shivered and looked back toward the ocean. "They are strangers."

"They're just boys who came to fix our boat so we can take it away. They go to school with me," she told him.

"School?" He brightened. "Then they do not come from San Marcos? They are not of the revolution?"

"Of course not!" she assured the boy. "Is San Marcos where you're from?"

"*Sí, señorita!* And some day when the wicked ones are driven out, we are going home again. *Mi abuelo* says the day comes soon when we—"

"Pablo!" It was Francisco Marino's voice calling harshly. He stood only a few feet away. "Go home to your *abuela* at once! She has been looking everywhere for you!"

6
Signals and Mystery

The elderly man's voice was harsh as he spoke to his grandson, and little Pablo looked frightened. Without a word, he ran off at once and disappeared behind the cottage.

Marino turned accusingly to Annette. "Why do you ask the boy questions?"

She was bewildered at his attitude and a little angry at being spoken to in that tone of voice. "I was trying to be friendly, Señor Marino."

Marino studied her sharply a moment, then he seemed to relax. He smiled apologetically. "A thousand pardons, child. My nerves are a little—what do you say—edged?"

"On edge," Annette supplied with a smile.

"Yes, on edge. That is the way to say it, thank you. You mean no harm, of course, but his grandmother and I try not to mention the things that have passed in our unfortunate country. There was much bloodshed and terror in the revolution, and the boy saw some of it. Now we try to make him forget." He sighed heavily as he finished.

"Oh, I'm sorry! I had no idea," Annette said contritely. "He's such a darling, I couldn't help making friends with him."

"I understand! It was kind of you," Señor Marino said quickly. "And now, the boat—it is ready to leave my cove soon?"

"They're working hard on it, but they're not very expert. It's taking them longer than they expected to replank it, I'm afraid," Annette said truthfully.

Marino's pleasant expression disappeared. He said abruptly with a scowl, "They must finish today and go. I told them yesterday what would happen to the boat if they did not." He was arrogant now, a man accustomed to giving orders and having them obeyed, Annette thought.

But he wasn't in his own country now. And she quietly told him, "I don't know how it is in

San Marcos, Señor Marino, but in this country the police look down upon people who deliberately destroy other people's property. If you sink that sailboat, they'll give you a lot of trouble. They might even put you in jail."

Marino looked thoughtful a moment, then nodded. "I see. That would be inconvenient, I'm afraid. I have some important business on hand and nothing must interfere with it."

"I'll do everything I can to hurry the boys," Annette promised. "They should be done and on their way home tomorrow, I'm positive."

"If it's the best they can do, I can't expect more," the elderly man said with a frown. "Very well. Tomorrow I shall hope to have my privacy again." With a courteous bow, the distinguished-looking artist strode away toward the studio barn. Annette hurried to tell the boys what had happened.

"Good gal!" Rod chuckled as Annette repeated her conversation with Marino.

"Just as well the old duck changed his mind about sinking this scow," Neil grumbled defiantly.

"I was planning to sleep aboard tonight in case he did try any monkey business."

"Then you aren't able to finish the repairs tonight?" She wasn't too surprised. "Good thing I had a hunch."

"Yeah, lucky," Rod agreed. "We accidentally split one of the new planks. Got to bring out another tomorrow. We had just tossed a coin to see who'd explain it to Marino when you brought the reprieve. For that, we now crown thee Queen of Smugglers' Cove." He bowed deeply and grinned.

Neil frowned impatiently. "Now we've got to get back to work, or we'll still be here on Saturday when you expect us to labor all day on that luau deal of yours." He shook a hammer playfully at her as she wrinkled her nose defiantly.

And with that, Annette was on her way up the narrow trail that led onto the headland south of the cove.

Among the trees was a wide patch of blue-flowered chicory, which boldly mingled its fragile, flat blossoms with the bright gold of the sunflowers. To her satisfaction, there was a wide view of the ocean, from the calm waters of the cove to the islands out in the channel. As she settled down comfortably in the shade of a poplar, she saw on the horizon the long trail of smoke from some passing freighter. She wondered where it was going and tried to imagine where it had been.

Her imagination was interrupted by the sound of a motorboat engine. She could not see it yet, but she could tell from the direction of the sound that it was south of the headland she was on. As it grew louder, she waited for it to cross the mouth of the cove and be visible.

When it did come into view a moment later, she gasped. It was undoubtedly the same little cruiser which had made the wake that had upset the sailboat! The orange sweater on the man at the wheel was unmistakable.

"Wish I had brought Rod's binoculars with me," she told herself impatiently. "I'd like to get a close look at that big ape. Wonder where the other fellow is?"

She didn't have to wonder long. The other man, the one who had sat in the cockpit yesterday, came out of the cabin with his binoculars and looked shoreward through them as the cruiser changed course and ran toward the beach. Almost instantly, he lowered the glasses and gave a quick order to his helmsman. Immediately, the helmsman swung the wheel, and the little cruiser made a wide arc and headed out toward the open sea. But once it was beyond the cove, the sound of the powerful motors stopped, and the cruiser lay to on the gently rolling swells.

Annette chuckled to herself. "Looks like they're not happy about the boys being on the beach. Well, they'll have themselves a long wait if they hang around out there hoping we will leave!"

The hammering down below had stopped, and Annette felt sure that the boys were watching the cruiser, too. I hope they can make out that number on her side, she thought. It's too far for me to see what it is. Once they had the registration number, they could check the list at the Coast

Guard station to find the owner. He might be persuaded to pay for those repairs, after all.

Annette gathered up the food she hadn't yet begun to eat and was about to stand up and start down the hill to check with Neil and Rod, when she noticed that the man in the cruiser was waving his arm to someone ashore. She felt sure it wasn't the boys he was greeting. For a moment she thought he might be waving to her. But that didn't make sense, because he seemed to be looking at some point on the other side of the cove.

She glanced across at the opposite hilltop. A man was standing there on a rock facing the ocean. It was Señor Marino. He was waving his arm at the man in the cruiser, and if she read his gestures correctly, he was warning the visitors to go away!

She took a hurried look toward the cruiser. The man with the binoculars was answering the signal with a vigorous nod and wave. Then he turned away, said something to the orange-sweatered helmsman, and went below. A moment later, the big motors roared again and

the cruiser took off, disappearing southward once more.

When Annette looked back toward the hill, the elderly painter had disappeared.

She hurried down to join the boys and tell them what she had seen. "Did you see that cruiser just now?" she demanded breathlessly.

"What about it?" Neil asked crossly. The interruption had made him hit his thumb for the third time that day and he was annoyed with the world.

"What are you steamed up about now?" Rod teased Annette.

"Those men in the cruiser! They were the same ones who came yesterday!" Annette announced excitedly, then told them about the signaling she had seen.

Neil threw down his hammer. "I wondered what was going on! I saw them maneuvering around out there. I'm going to talk to Marino and get the name of that guy in the cruiser!"

"I don't think he'll give it to you," Annette said soberly. "It looked to me as if he didn't want you to meet the 'guy' for some reason."

Neil looked grim. "Covering for him so he wouldn't get a punch in the jaw for wrecking our boat. Well, old Marino's going to tell us who he is, or I'll—" He stopped with a growl, doubling his fist.

"Better not tangle with him. We're not ready to pull out just yet," Rod advised. "I have a hunch that cruiser will be around again tomorrow and we may get a better look at its license number. All I saw this time was 'A35'—I missed the rest because a wave broke just then and covered it. Once we have that number, we can trace the owner ourselves."

"Okay," Neil said reluctantly, "but if they don't show up tomorrow, I'm going to take it up with Marino."

When Annette drove the boys back to Smugglers' Cove the next morning, however, they saw no signs of the Marinos about the little cottage. And though it took almost the whole morning to put the new plank in place, they still had not had a glimpse of either the Marinos or the small cruiser by the time the job was done.

They loaded a borrowed pair of oars into the sloop and pushed the small boat out through the surf. Rod climbed in and rowed around a little while Neil and Annette watched.

"Okay," he called from a few yards out, "not a leak! Let's go, boy! We've got a long row ahead of us."

"Right with you!" Neil answered.

"Aren't you going to dive and try to find the goggles and fins we lost the other day?" Annette asked. "You brought those borrowed ones along, and I thought you were planning—"

"We changed our minds," Neil explained. "By now, the stuff you lost overboard two days ago could be anywhere on the bottom of the cove or outside it. We'll just add the cost of it to the bill we'll hand to Marino's friend when we find out who he is."

"If we ever do," Annette told herself silently. She felt pretty sure that Marino would not be very willing to give them any information about the men in the cruiser.

"It's too bad you didn't bring your scuba equipment," she told the boys. "You could really explore the place and at the same time gather us some abalones and crabs to cook Saturday night for the luau."

"Hey! That isn't a bad idea!" Neil beamed. "Maybe we'll sail back and do that tomorrow afternoon, if we get the new mast stepped in early enough, and the sail rigged."

"Marino may kick up a fuss if we show up again," Rod suggested doubtfully.

"There's no reason why we have to anchor in this cove," Neil argued. "We can drop anchor in the next bay and swim back here under-water to look for that stuff. He doesn't have to see us at all."

"That's right," Rod agreed. "We can keep an eye out for the cruiser while we're at it."

Annette watched Neil swim out to the sloop and climb aboard. She called, "I'll be watching at the dock!" As Rod began the long row back, she went up the canyon to the end of the old road where the Monster was parked.

As Annette went past the cottage and the barn, she saw no sign of life. Three picture books that she had brought for Pablo were still on the front step of the cottage. She hoped he would like them.

She went on to her car without suspecting that behind the drawn curtains of the cottage Señor Marino was telling his wife, "Good! Now they are gone, and we shall not see them again!"

7

Some Surprises

Annette could hardly wait to tell Babs about the mysterious goings-on between Francisco Marino and the two men in the cruiser. She hastily parked her car in the McCleods' garage and dashed into the house.

Aunt Lila was finishing one of the colorful costumes Annette and Babs intended to wear at the luau. They were of vivid Hawaiian-printed cotton with big splashy hibiscus flowers all over. Annette's was bright red, and Babs's was sky blue.

"You're just in time to try this on," Aunt Lila told Annette, "if you want to."

"Oh, I'm sure it's just perfect, Aunt Lila. And you're a darling to make it for me!" She gave Aunt Lila a quick hug. "I want to talk to Babs. Is she better?"

Aunt Lila chuckled. "Practically well, but still sniffling a little. I think she'll live."

Babs was sitting up in bed, still surrounded by fashion magazines and movie-fan publications. She greeted Annette excitedly. "Wait till you see what I've found out!" She waved a large fashion magazine at Annette. "I just *knew* he would turn out to be somebody!"

"Who, for goodness' sake?" Annette asked.

"That good-looking Mr. Horton, of course! The one we saw with your uncle last night!" She thrust the magazine at Annette. "Here! Read about him!"

Annette sat on the edge of the bed and looked at the full-page photograph of the handsome young man. It had been taken against the background of the reception hall in the presidential palace of his father, the exiled ruler of San Marcos. Under the picture the caption read, "'Don Venustiano de Marino Melendez y Horton, affectionately known to his friends as Tino.'" Annette read it aloud, stumbling over the pronunciation of the names.

"With that string of names, no wonder he calls himself Tino Horton!" Annette laughed.

"Isn't he marvelous?" Babs clasped her hands together and rolled her eyes romantically skyward. "And to think, he lives only a few houses up the strand now!"

"I hope you're not intending to invite him to our luau," Annette told her. "I have an idea he wouldn't be the least bit interested in such kid stuff."

"I don't see why not," Babs said, pouting.

"Because he's entirely out of our class. He's older, for one thing. Practically ancient. You saw that yourself last night. And you read what it says here in the magazine. 'His amusing parties were the talk of Paris and Monte Carlo while his father was president of San Marcos, and the gaming tables of Europe surely must miss him. But their loss is Las Vegas's gain during his frequent visits from his new home in sunny California! Good luck, Tino the Great!' Does that sound as if he'd have a gorgeous time at our poor little beach blast?"

"Oh, I suppose not," Babs said with a sigh, "but he's awfully cute!"

Annette was reading on. "'His father is living in exile on a small rancho on the coast of San Pascual, the country next to San Marcos.'" She paused. "Oh, this isn't fair! It says that San Marcos's new regime is accusing ex-President Melendez of stealing because he took some of the family's heirlooms with him when he fled during the revolution. They're trying to make San Pascual seize them from him. Isn't that disgusting? But I guess that's just politics."

"I suppose so," Babs agreed. Then she tossed her blond curls. "Anyhow, I think Tino's dashing. And I'd like to have his autograph. So there!" A moment later she clapped her hands excitedly. "I know what we'll do! We'll walk past his house and see if he's around. Maybe he'd like to have a copy of this magazine—if he hasn't seen it yet."

"Ha!" Annette hooted. "He probably has dozens of copies!"

"Well, anyhow, let's stroll down that way.

Aunt Lila said I could go for a walk with you if the sun was still up when you got home. And it is!"

Annette didn't feel much like walking after her busy day, but Babs was already out of bed and getting into her clothes.

"Okay, but we're not going to take him that magazine or gawk at him. We'll simply walk past and peek over the hedge. If he's there and happens to look at you, please don't swoon!"

"Of course not!" Babs answered with great dignity. Then as she studied her face in the mirror, she groaned. "Oh, dear! My poor nose is so red. Do you think that he'll notice?"

"He probably won't even be there. And if he is, maybe he's too nearsighted to see!" Annette teased. "Be calm!"

"I'll bet you're the one who'll do flip-flops if he gives you a smile like this one in the picture and maybe kisses your hand!"

"I don't intend to get close enough to find out," Annette said pertly with a sniff of disdain. "Come on. It's almost sundown, and if you don't hurry, Aunt Lila won't let you out of the house with those sniffles."

They strolled along the beach walk toward the big Garrett place nearly a block away. A couple of the houses in between were dark and empty. Their owners had gone back to town for the winter. But a few were still occupied, and the girls exchanged greetings with several of their invited luau guests as they went by.

At the boardinghouse where both Neil and Rod were living, the landlady was out sweeping sand off the walk.

"Rod and Neil may be late for dinner, Mrs. Polk," Annette told her. "They said to tell you."

"If those two rascals think I'm keeping their food hot while they sail merrily around the ocean, they're in for a surprise," Mrs. Polk announced, waving the broom fiercely.

"But the poor kids aren't sailing, Mrs. Polk. They're rowing that sailboat from a long way off. They'll be dead tired when they come in," Annette pleaded, "and simply *famished*!"

Mrs. Polk sighed. "I guess, if that's the case,

I could keep something warm for them."

"Oh, thanks, Mrs. Polk," Annette said grate-fully. "That'll be wonderful."

As they went on toward the Garrett place, Babs giggled and looked admiringly at Annette. "You know very well they're probably stuffing themselves with all those sandwiches and the cake Aunt Lila packed for you."

"Oh, well, they always have room for more!" Annette said lightly.

They were coming to the Garrett place. A tall hedge surrounded the wide lawn, and there were bright zinnias in bloom all along the path up to the two-story house. A lawn sprinkler was whirling.

The girls peered over the hedge, standing on tiptoe.

"Nobody around," Babs said with a sigh after a long look.

"Well, we tried any—" Annette broke off to stare at the figure in the doorway, wearing khaki shorts and an orange sweater. "Look, Babs! It's the fellow who was steering that cruiser."

Babs looked, and then they ducked down.

"If *he* lives here with Mr. Horton, then the second man in the cruiser could have been—" Babs's whisper broke off as they heard two men's voices speaking Spanish. One of them was smooth and melodious, the same voice Annette had heard when Tino Horton was talking with Uncle Archie.

Annette braved a quick peek over the hedge. "It *was*! There he is now, talking to the big brute. And he's wearing that yachting cap, just as he was in the cruiser when he nearly drowned us!" She took Babs by the arm. "Come on home," she whispered. "I'm going to tell Uncle Archie and have him get after Mr. Tino Horton for the repairs to the sailboat."

Babs held back, whispering in protest. "Wait. You told me Uncle Archie said that maybe they didn't even know they had upset us."

"He doesn't think so, but I do," Annette said with a frown. "And they should at least get a good talking-to for being so careless. Maybe if they do, Mr. Horton will be ashamed of himself

and offer to pay the bill for the repairs without being asked."

"I'm sure he will," Babs said with a final admiring look over the hedge.

Annette had not noticed the small cruiser tied up beside the Garrett dock when they had arrived. Now, as they started back down the strand, she saw it. It was covered with a tarpaulin but she felt sure it was the one that had carried the men to Smugglers' Cove.

"Wait a sec," she told Babs hastily and ran lightly out on the dock to investigate. As she had suspected, the registry number hidden under the tarp was one that began with "A35," the three symbols Rod had read on the offending cruiser.

She hurriedly rejoined Babs, and they went back to report the discovery to Uncle Archie. But Uncle Archie let them know promptly that he had no intention of mentioning the matter to Mr. Horton. Yes, he knew who the young man really was. And he respected his wish to be anonymous. "Poor fellow has had enough publicity," he told them. As for informing Mr. Horton of the accident and hoping he'd offer to pay for the damages, that was out.

There was no more to be said about the matter. "You are just lucky you didn't do more damage to Neil's borrowed sailboat," Uncle Archie said in concluding their discussion.

It was quite late in the night when Annette, still fully dressed, waited at her window, watching for the sloop. The night air was very still, and the waves lapped gently against the shore. She was on the verge of falling asleep when she heard the sound of oars. Out at the end of the dock, a small boat nosed up against the pilings. Two tired young men climbed out and tied up their craft.

Annette ran swiftly downstairs and out to greet them.

"Thank goodness, you got here!" she exclaimed. "I was so worried. I thought of all sorts of things that might have happened, like the boat's leaking."

Rod laughed. "We're better carpenters than that, madam. It was our blisters that slowed us down." He showed blistered palms, and so did Neil. But Neil wasn't laughing. He couldn't even smile. He was in a foul mood.

"Come on, let's turn in," he barked at Rod. "We've got more labor ahead of us tomorrow, thanks to our pal here."

Annette looked unhappy, and Rod saw it. "Don't rub it in, fella," he said quietly. "Save your mad for the guys who really did the damage, those two cruiserites."

Annette exclaimed, "Oh! I forgot! What I really stayed up for was to tell you that Babs and I found out who those men are. They live right up the strand at the Garrett place. We saw them there tonight. And the cruiser's tied up at the dock!"

Neil growled angrily. "Great! I'll just go by there now and have a little talk with those guys!"

"Oh, no, Neil! Uncle Archie says we're not to bother Mr. Horton about the accident. He says I'm still the one who's responsible for the damage because I had no right to take the boat," Annette explained. "He says—"

Neil interrupted with a scowl. "I don't care what your uncle says," he said rudely. "Those jokers did the damage, and they're going to pay the bills."

"You can't go barging into a guy's house at this time of night," Rod protested. "Let's get through here and hit the hay. I'm all in, and so are you."

But Neil didn't wait to hear Rod's protest. He spun on his heel and stalked off the dock.

"Oh, dear!" Annette cried unhappily. "Can't you stop him somehow? I didn't mean to start anything."

Rod frowned after the tall young athlete disappearing up the beach walk. "He'll cool off by the time he gets to the Garretts', but I suppose I'd better go after him as soon as I cover the boat and stow these tools."

8

Special Delivery

It took only a few minutes for Rod to make the sailboat secure for the night. Then he hurried Annette to her door.

"Take it easy," he told her. "Quit worrying about what Neil will do. His temper disappears as fast as it comes. By now, he's probably on his way back to our diggings after giving Horton a couple of dirty looks." He chuckled. "He has *some* sense, you know."

"Oh, I hope so!" Annette felt reassured. "See you in the morning." She opened the door and went in.

Rod hurried away up the strand. He paused in front of the boardinghouse and looked up at Neil's window, half expecting to see a light already there. But the room was as dark as the rest of the house, and Rod went on.

He had reached the end of the hedge shielding the Garrett grounds from the view of passersby when he heard a rough voice exclaim in Spanish, "Go and do not return or Señor Horton will inform the police of your intrusion!"

The voice came from the other side of the hedge. Neil's voice answered angrily. "I'm not going till I talk to your boss, bud. So, just get out of my—ow!" Rod heard a blow and a groan.

He decided it was time for him to make a move. He strode hastily toward the gate halfway along the hedge. But before he could reach it, two tall figures came through the gate. The bigger one was half carrying the other, who was wobbly-legged. Neil was the groggy one. Rod could see that much even in the semidarkness.

When the man holding Neil up saw Rod hurrying toward him, he let go of Neil, who slumped against the hedge, holding his jaw and looking dazed.

"Hey! What's the idea?" Rod demanded as he approached.

The big man reached into his pocket and

brought out a revolver. He held it lightly and didn't point it at Rod, but Rod got the message. "You don't have to get rough!" Rod was annoyed to find his voice quavering a little in spite of his effort to make it sound as tough as the other man's.

The tall man laughed and pocketed the gun as he said sternly, "Take your *amigo* away before I forget you are children and call your police to arrest you for the invasion of Señor Horton's estate. Here!" He grasped Neil's arm suddenly and pushed him toward Rod. "Away! Both of you!"

They collided and nearly knocked each other down. When they gathered their wits and looked for him, he had disappeared through the gate.

"I'll show that gorilla!" Neil fumed, and he started toward the gate to follow him. Rod gripped his arm and held on.

"You've done enough for one night. Come on," Rod told him quietly, and Neil went with him meekly back along the walk. He had nothing to say as they walked around to the back of the boardinghouse, let themselves in quietly, and tiptoed across the kitchen in darkness.

They were both hungry, and they looked longingly at the closed door of Mrs. Polk's refrigerator. Her boarders were strictly forbidden to raid its sacred contents, but it was a temptation. They looked at each other sadly, and then Rod whispered, "No use thinking about it. Polkie would never forgive us!" Neil nodded glumly and they tiptoed toward the hall door.

But as Rod reached out to push the door open, he felt a sheet of paper pinned to it. He lit a match to read the message. "It's from Polkie," he said in a stage whisper. "She says dinner's in the oven. 'Please wash dishes and silver. Milk in fridge. One glass each, please. Eliza Polk.'" He switched on the lights, and both of them dashed to look inside the oven.

Dinner was there, as the note said. Two heaping platefuls of it, wrapped in aluminum foil and pleasantly hot. "How nice!" Rod sighed as he took his food to the table. Neil agreed heartily.

Neil hadn't told him yet just what had

happened on the Horton lawn, so Rod hesitated to ask. Then he noticed that a black-and-blue mark was showing on Neil's jaw. "Boy!" he exclaimed. "He really socked you, that guy!"

"Yeah," Neil said with a growl, feeling his jaw. "He has a fist like a hammer. Caught me unaware. I heard voices out by the garage and it sounded like an argument. So I went nosing around back there to take a look."

"And ran into Junior, huh?"

"Uh-uh," Neil said, shaking his head emphatically. "Not right then. I got an earful first."

"Anything exciting? Or was it all in Spanish?"

"That's the funny part," Neil admitted. "The only one of the three guys there that even had an accent was Horton. The other two were something right out of a cops-and-robbers movie on *The Late Show*, tough but cool."

"What was the argument?" Rod asked.

"It was something about Horton giving somebody in Las Vegas a bad check. The guys were promising him a lot of trouble if he didn't make good."

"What did he say to that?" Rod asked eagerly.

"He said he had made arrangements that would more than take care of his small debt." Neil scowled. "I don't know if they believed him, but anyhow I decided he had had enough trouble for one night, and I started to leave. I got as far as the gate and I changed my mind. If he can pay off something big like that bad check must be, it won't hurt him to pay a hundred bucks to fix up the boat."

"Makes sense," Rod agreed. "So you went back—"

"I started back, but this big ape grabbed me and—I guess you heard the rest," he concluded, feeling his sore jaw and glowering.

"I suppose we could stop by there in the morning," Rod said doubtfully, "but maybe we'd better just let it slide." Seeing Neil frown, he added, "For now."

"Yeah," Neil agreed, scowling, "for now. But I'm not giving up. The more I hear about this Horton, the less I think of him."

"Maybe we can collar him if he happens to go by while we're working on the boat tomorrow at the McCleods'," Rod suggested.

"You can bet on it. I'll be watching for him!" Neil said grimly.

But the next morning, even after the new mast had been stepped in and the sail rigged, there had been no sign of either Tino Horton or the big man who worked for him. And the little cruiser lay under its tarpaulin at the Garrett dock.

For all they knew, Tino Horton might have had to leave for Las Vegas with the two threatening messengers.

"Good breeze up," Rod commented as they put away the tools and admired their finished job. "Why don't we pull out while it's blowing? It won't take us long to load on the scuba stuff and then off we go!"

"Good idea," said Annette's voice. "And in case you weren't going to invite me along, I'm going just the same. I'm paying my way with this basketful of goodies for lunch. Invited?"

"And how!" Rod laughed. "Always room for one more—lunch basket, that is."

"What are you going to do with those picture books?" Neil asked as Annette started to come aboard.

"They're for Pablo," she explained. "An American history and an animal book. Mostly pictures."

"You're forgetting we haven't planned to stop at the cove," Neil said impatiently. "We're going to anchor in the next one and swim back underwater to look for that stuff you managed to lose for us."

"I know that," Annette said coldly, "but you could let me off at Smugglers' Cove on the beach and then go to the other place."

"And risk running this boat on the rocks again?" Neil growled. "Nothing doing. Why can't you drive over?"

"Thanks for the kind suggestion. Maybe that's just what I'll do!" Annette said tersely. She reached down and picked up the lunch basket and started to leave.

"Hey, where are you going with the lunch?" Rod asked quickly, alarmed.

"I'm sure little Pablo will enjoy it with me," she said with a toss of her head.

"Aw, wait, Annette! Look, you come along with us. We'll let you out in shallow water, and you can wade ashore. Then we'll sail around to the next cove and do our diving like we planned. We'll pick you up when we're through diving. How's that?" Rod coaxed.

"A-okay, since you've invited me so politely," Annette said saucily and sat down in the sloop. "Now, tell me how you made out with Mr. Tino Horton last night."

Neil was sulky, but Rod gave her the details quickly. She was sympathetic, but she couldn't help feeling that Neil had earned his sore jaw by acting without thinking.

She was wise enough not to say so, though.

She waded ashore in Smugglers' Cove, carrying her beach shoes and the books on her head. When she reached the dry sand, she waited to watch the sailboat disappear around the north point. Then she went on up the canyon.

At first she thought there was no one at home. Then, as she turned to leave when her second knock went unanswered, the door opened abruptly, and Señora Marino, looking rather worried, appeared.

"I've brought Pablo some more books," Annette began with a smile.

"He is not here. I will take them, señorita. And thank you," the elderly woman said hastily. "But if you do not mind, please go away at once. There is someone who comes to see my husband on very important business."

"Of course, I don't mind!" Annette said quickly. Then she thought, A customer for a painting probably!

Señora Marino gave a quick little pat to Annette's arm. "You come *mañana*—that is tomorrow, yes?"

"I'll try," Annette promised cheerfully. "Say hello to Pablo and I hope he likes the books." She started away and heard the door close quickly after her. As she went down the canyon toward the beach, she wondered what she was going to do with herself till the boys sailed back to pick her up.

It was low tide and the sun was warm on the sand. She stretched out between two big rocks and watched tiny waves curl around the edges of the bay. She was half asleep when she heard the sound of a plane engine. She turned over lazily and looked up at the sky to see what kind it was. Probably a Coast Guard patrol, she decided.

But it was a private plane that came in high and made wide circles over the cove. Then it made a low pass over the cove and darted away to the south again.

A minute later, Annette heard a familiar sound, and Tino Horton, with his helmsman at the wheel, came into sight around the headland in the little cruiser.

"So, you're the customer—the important customer—that Señor Marino is expecting," Annette told him, from a half mile away. "I hope he charges you a nice fat price to make a portrait of you that looks like a fried egg!"

But the cruiser made no attempt to land Horton. Instead, the helmsman turned off the motor, and the small craft sat out in the seaway, bobbing on the swells.

Suddenly, the plane was back, and Horton was waving to the pilot as the machine circled high over the cove.

Annette watched, puzzled. Then she saw something being tossed out of the plane and falling toward the water. While the object was still in the air, the plane took off and disappeared to the south.

And suddenly, the falling package opened out into a parachute with something that looked like a long metal cylinder hanging from it.

9

What Is in It?

Annette watched intently from her spot on the sand between the rocks as the parachute descended. She tried to keep as hidden as possible, in case either Tino Horton or his helmsman should happen to glance shoreward.

But she needn't have worried about being seen just then. Both men in the small cruiser were too intent on watching the swaying descent of the parachute to notice anything else. They had started up the cruiser's motors and were headed toward the spot where the metal cylinder seemed likely to strike the water.

Halfway to the surface of the water, the parachute was caught by a brisk gust of wind and went sailing madly off at an angle that would bring it down well aft of the cruiser.

Before the helmsman could change his course,

the cylinder and parachute struck the waves and disappeared momentarily underwater. By the time the cruiser reached the spot, the parachute had risen to the surface and was floating.

Tino Horton took the wheel as the helmsman leaned over the rail with a grappling hook and drew the parachute to him while the motors idled.

Annette squinted at the distant scene and felt a bit disappointed when she saw that the big man was recovering the fallen parachute. "I hoped you'd fall overboard, you big bully!" she said out loud severely. "Would have served you right for hitting Neil so hard last night."

But her disappointment vanished as she saw there was no metal cylinder attached to the cords of the parachute. "Oh, good! They've lost it!"

She chuckled to herself as she saw the big man peel off his orange sweater and go over the rail into the choppy waves. She could see, even at this distance, that the cruiser had drifted quite a way from the spot where the parachute had hit the water. It would be hard to find the missing cylinder, for that was deep water and there were probably a lot of rocks on the floor of the cove.

Now the helmsman was coming up. He was empty-handed. Tino Horton was waving his arms and shouting at him. The big man was waving his own arms and arguing back, but after a moment he dived out of sight again.

"Har, har! Hope you don't find it!" Annette giggled. She was still being very careful not to sit up and be seen. She felt sure that Mr. Horton would not be happy if he suspected that he was being watched. Whatever this mysterious attempt to deliver something to him meant, it was probably very secret. And it could have something to do with that conversation Neil had heard last night— the conversation between Tino and the two hard-looking men about an arrangement Tino had made that would take care of his Las Vegas debt.

Now the helmsman was up again, shaking his head over his failure to locate the metal cylinder. He was gasping for breath and hanging on to the side of the cruiser rather limply. But Tino Horton was pointing to the water and seemed to be insisting that he try again.

The argument ended suddenly as the sailboat came nosing around the point, tacking for shore. The boys were in their swimming trunks as Rod handled the tiller and Neil posed beside the mast.

The cruiser's motors roared and the swimmer scrambled hastily aboard and took the wheel from Tino Horton. A moment later, the cruiser was heading rapidly south to disappear around the headland.

The two boys stared after it. They had both recognized the big man, but it wasn't till after they had picked up Annette that they found out what the men had been trying to do.

"Looks like we scared them off." Neil jeered. Then he looked thoughtful. "You're sure they didn't find that cylinder thing?"

"Positive," Annette assured him. "And by the time they come back with skin-diving gear to look for it, the undertow may have buried it under tons of sand, so they'll never find it!"

"It would serve them right," Neil said shortly.

But Rod told them, "If it was as big a thing as you say, Annette, it might take more than one tide to cover it. They still have a chance of finding it if they don't wait too long to come back."

"I imagine they'll wait till they're sure you're not still hanging around to watch," Annette said.

"I wonder what's in it," Rod said, peering over the side of the sloop into the deep water but catching no glimpse of the missing cylinder.

"Hey!" Neil had a sudden idea. "Why don't we slip back into our scuba outfits and dive for it ourselves?"

"What makes you want to do that pair any favor?" Rod asked, puzzled. "Specially after the big guy clobbered you last night for nothing?"

"Because I'm a good-hearted Joe, that's why!" Neil grinned broadly and then added with a glance at Annette, "Even if some people think I'm a total loss!"

Annette flushed. It was almost as if Neil had read her mind as she was thinking, That doesn't sound like Neil, doing favors for anybody!

Rod said hastily, "Come off it! Nobody thinks that, Neil. It's just that, well, I'd never peg you for the forgiving type—that's for sure!"

"Shows how little some people know about a guy," Neil said with a growl. "Let's drag out that gear again."

Rod went forward to the locker, but as he laid back the lid, he stopped suddenly and laughed. "Hey, we both forgot something. We're almost out of air in the tanks. Remember? That's why we gave up looking for our goggles."

"Oh, yeah," Neil said, scowling. "Well, let's pull out of here. Maybe we'll come by here tomorrow and see what's going on."

They were soon underway with Neil at the tiller and Rod handling the sail expertly. Annette sat in the bow and enjoyed the breeze that took them rapidly out toward the jutting headland.

Just before they reached it, Annette looked back toward the beach. Señor Marino and Pablo were standing there, watching.

"There's Señor Marino," she told the boys. "I guess he may have been waiting for that plane to drop its load, too." Then she waved gaily to the pair on shore.

Marino turned away abruptly and started up

into the canyon, but the youngster jumped up and down and waved excitedly with the book that he was carrying. He pointed to the book and then hugged it. His meaning was clear. He was saying thanks for it.

Tino Horton and Señor Marino certainly seem to be in it together, whatever it is that's going on, she thought. Maybe there's money in that cylinder. Maybe it's for a revolution to restore the *ex-presidente*. But, if they *were* plotting something, and the cylinder was important to them, it certainly was nothing that concerned herself or the two boys. She hoped that Neil wouldn't get himself and Rod mixed up in it by coming back tomorrow and trying to help find the thing.

Rod's voice cut into her thoughts. "Why is the Queen of Smugglers' Cove looking so sad? Is it because we have failed to bring her abalones for her luau?"

"Well, we could use them and we wouldn't have to make so many hamburgers," she said frankly. "But mostly, I guess, I was thinking about all the work that we still have to do to get ready for the party. It's only a day after tomorrow, and if you boys are out here underwater all day hunting for that cylinder, which is probably way out in the seaway by now, it's going to be hard for us girls—"

"Whoa, sis!" Neil cut in, laughing. "You're running out of breath. Calm yourself. We have the answer."

"Oh, good!" Annette gave him a smile. "You're going to forget all about looking for that silly cylinder!"

"How did you guess?" Neil grinned. "We're wiping it right off the blackboard. But we're going to get you those abalones, just as we set out to do. And we're going to do it tonight! Rod, you remember that big pile of rocks close to the point? I'm sure that's a prime spot for abalones. We'll take an underwater spotlight and our own waterproof flashlights."

"That's a great idea!" Rod agreed. "I went night diving in Hawaii but I haven't tried it here. It's a real gasser walking around on the bottom of the ocean at night. Kinda spooky, though. Things sure look weird."

"We'll take along our spears and diving knives in case any angry octopuses don't like our waking them up in the middle of the night!" Neil laughed.

"It sounds pretty dangerous to me," Annette said, objecting.

"I thought you wanted abalones," Neil said shortly.

"We do, but—" she hesitated.

"There's really no danger," Rod assured her quickly. "We'll drop anchor near the point, and we'll tie one of the flashes to the anchor chain to guide us back to the boat with our sackful."

"Suppose Tino Horton comes back looking for his cylinder? Won't he think you're looking for it, too?" Annette asked. "He won't like it."

Rod and Neil both laughed. "Not a chance of his coming. He has no idea you saw it fall," Neil said, "and we were underwater in the next cove when the plane that dropped it went over."

Annette felt relieved, especially when Rod

added, "Whatever jam he's in with the gamblers up at Las Vegas about the check, it can't be so urgent that he'd have to have that cylinder tonight. Even if it's filled with money!"

"Hey, why don't you and Babs come along with us tonight? We can bring the guitar and do some practicing for Saturday night as we sail," Neil suggested. "Then, if Horton did come by, he wouldn't get the crazy idea that we were after his stuff. He'd know that it was just a sailing party."

"That might be fun!" Annette agreed. "I'll see if Babs is over the sniffles and if Aunt Lila will give us permission to go."

"Great! And when we get back to Laguna with our abalones, we can have coffee and doughnuts at your house while we dig out the abalone steaks and get them pounded and ready for cooking. They won't be quite so tough if they have a few extra hours in the fridge." Rod had experience with abalone. He knew that unless the tasty shellfish meat was properly prepared, it would be like leather.

Aunt Lila was not so sure that the girls should go sailing in the night air, but they talked her into it.

"But take wraps along, both of you. You know how chilly it gets on the water so late in the summer," she warned them. "And home by ten at the latest."

They assured her they'd be prompt and then dashed upstairs to change and get ready for an early dinner.

As they joined Neil and Rod in the sloop, the sunset was tinging the waters a gentle pink. And an hour later, as the moon was rising majestically full over Smugglers' Cove, the little sailboat rode at anchor near the rocks of the north boundary of the cove.

Down below, a faint light shimmered from the waterproof flashlight tied to the anchor chain. There was no sign of the boys, who had gone overboard in their full scuba equipment, armed with spears, knives, and spotlight some ten minutes before.

"I could fall asleep," Babs said, yawning as the long glassy swells lifted the small boat and floated it idly, its sail hanging limply.

"Sh-h-h!" Annette laid a hand on her arm. "Look! Somebody's coming!"

10

Neil Makes Plans

In the bright moonlight, they could see a man's figure in a small skiff that was approaching from the direction of the beach.

For a moment, Annette felt a sinking of her heart. If this was Tino Horton arriving and the boys came to the surface while he was here, there might very well be trouble. He would be sure to think they had come to look for the cylinder and might be very disagreeable.

But as the small boat came closer, she could see that the man hunched over at the oars was a shorter, heavier man. Then the moonlight revealed that it was the elderly painter Francisco Marino.

"Hi, there!" Babs waved a friendly greeting. But Marino gave no sign that he had heard her. He rowed up to them before he spoke.

"What are you doing here at this hour of the night?" he demanded crossly. "This is no place for young ladies to be alone."

"We're not alone, Señor Marino," Annette told him quietly. "The rest of the party is down there." She pointed to the faintly glimmering flashlight below on the anchor chain.

"Those two again? Why do they come here with you? What are they looking for? Speak up!" he commanded sharply.

"Abalones—" Annette said with a smile, "for a little party that Babs and I are giving on Saturday night. A Hawaiian luau. At our house in Laguna."

"Abalones?" The elderly man frowned uncertainly. Then he asked suspiciously, "What are they?"

"Like big clams, only rough on the outside and with the most beautiful mother-of-pearl lining inside the shells. We're going to eat the clammy part at the luau and hang the shells on fishnet so the lights will reflect on them, and—"

Marino cut her short. "Charming, señorita, I

am sure. But why do you come here to my cove for these clams, or whatever you call them, when there must be many other places they can be found? I thought it was understood that there would be no more intrusions on my privacy."

"I'm sorry, Señor Marino, but all the little bays closer to Laguna have been cleaned out of abalones. This one seemed the most promising to the boys," Annette hurriedly explained.

"How long do you stay here? When will they be ready to depart?" he demanded, frowning.

"Any time now, I'm sure," Annette told him, looking down into the water hopefully but seeing no trace of the boys. "If there are any legal-sized abalones, they should have found them by now. They were planning to try one special spot in the rocks near here."

"Here's one of them now!" Babs called out excitedly, leaning over the side and pointing down at a light that was approaching the anchor chain where the underwater flashlight was tied. "Guess they got a load."

"Or none!" Annette laughed.

A moment later, as Rod rose to the surface in his wet suit and face mask, his tank on his back, he threw a well-filled burlap sack into the sloop before he hoisted himself aboard.

Babs grabbed for the sack and pulled it open. There were a dozen fine big abalones inside. She picked one up and showed it triumphantly to Marino. "Abalones! And are they ever yummy if you cook them right!"

"I'm sure we could spare a couple of your own abalones, Señor Marino," Annette said with a smile, "if you think Señora Marino would like to cook them. They're really delicious eating."

"Thank you, but no, señoritas," he said with the first sign of a smile they had seen on his face. Then he turned to Rod and asked sharply, "The other one, your friend, he comes up soon?"

Rod hesitated, to Annette's surprise. Then he said, "Oh, yeah. Any minute." He looked down into the water. "Here he comes now. He's just switched off the guide light."

Marino watched silently as Neil came to the surface beside the sloop. When Neil threw a half-filled sack of abalones into the boat, Marino's eyes searched it keenly. Then, as Neil climbed into the sloop and took off his hood and mask, Marino said, "It would be well to continue with your fishing elsewhere now. I have already explained that I am one who prefers solitude."

Annette saw Neil stiffen and scowl, and she thought, Oh, dear! Here comes an argument! But to her amazement, Neil suddenly relaxed and smiled at Marino.

"Sorry we bothered you again, Señor Marino, but I figured that bunch of rocks at the corner would be just the right place to get abalones, and I was almost right. There were some, but not many. We'll try some other place tomorrow."

Marino nodded. "I am sorry my cove was not more generous with its abalones, young man. And now, you go?"

"Soon as we shed these suits. They feel great while you're in the water but a little too warm and heavy out of it."

Marino nodded. Then he bent to the oars,

called a good night to them, and rowed slowly shoreward.

Annette eyed Neil curiously. He had been strangely amiable to Marino. She knew he had resented Marino's practically telling them to get out. He had stiffened and glared. And then he had been sweet as molasses to the painter. It was puzzling.

She had her answer a couple of minutes later. The moment that Marino was halfway to the beach in his skiff, Neil hastily put on his hood and face mask again and, without an explanation, slipped over the bow of the sloop and disappeared underwater.

Annette looked inquiringly at Rod. To her surprise, he had a frown on his face as he quickly avoided her eyes.

"Why, where's he going now?" Babs asked.

Rod didn't answer. Instead, he moved to the bow quickly as the anchor chain slackened and rattled. He started to haul it up. The unlit flashlight came into view first. Then, as Neil surfaced, all three of them saw that he was bringing

up a metal cylinder about a yard long and a foot in diameter which was still attached to the anchor chain by a length of seaweed.

As he gained the surface and lifted the cylinder for Rod to grasp and haul into the boat, Neil unwound the seaweed and cast it off.

Babs squealed. "Whatever is that?"

But Annette didn't have to ask. She knew. And she knew something else, too. She knew that Neil had come back here "for abalones," intending to find that cylinder, no matter what he had told her and Babs about it. It was like Neil. But the worst of it all was that she would never have expected Rod to be a party to it. She glared at him in disgust.

Rod caught her glance and looked grim. He had already taken off his wet suit as Neil started to climb back into the sailboat, and he went over to help his friend in safely.

The moment Neil had taken off his face mask, he grinned triumphantly at Annette and Babs and announced, "Well, there it is!"

Annette frowned at him. "So I see," she said

coldly. "It's what you really were looking for, isn't it? Not abalones."

Neil laughed, but Rod protested. "That's not so, Annette. We just spotted it down between two rocks, by accident. Didn't we, Neil?"

Neil shrugged. "Speak for yourself, bud. Sure, *you* weren't looking for it, but *I* was! As a matter of fact, kids, I had a pretty good idea where the riptide in this crummy cove would take it. I did a lot of skin diving around here this summer with the guys while you were in Hawaii, Rod, and we learned a lot about tides."

"I see you did," Rod said quietly. "Well, now you've recovered Mr. Horton's property, what are you going to do with it?"

Annette spoke quickly, "Hand it over to him, of course. Aren't you, Neil?"

Neil frowned. "I'll have to think about it first. Seems to me Horton owes me something for the sock on the jaw his oversized pal gave me. Maybe I'll do a bit of bargaining."

"But that doesn't seem honest to me," Babs objected. "There must be something important sealed in that thing, or Señor Marino wouldn't be rowing around in the middle of the night worrying about what you were diving for."

"Yeah," Neil picked up the metal cylinder and weighed it in his hands. "Could be most anything. Like money or jewelry. And with both Marino and Horton mixed up in the case, it could have something to do with politics in San Marcos." He looked at the sealed cap at one end. "I'd sure like to look inside."

"Hey, wait! These guys aren't playing games. You break into that and you'll find yourself in the middle," Rod warned. "They can claim you took part of it if anything's missing."

Neil laid down the cylinder hastily. "Don't get in an uproar. I'm not going to open it. I'm just going to keep it tucked away for a day or so, till Horton's guard, or whatever he is, gets tired of diving around looking for it. Then I'm going to pretend that we just accidentally found it. He ought to be ready to come through with a neat reward by that time."

"You know, he might, at that," Rod agreed

reluctantly. "But if he suspects any tricks, look out for rough stuff."

"I still think you should give it to Mr. Horton or Señor Marino the first thing in the morning," Annette said stubbornly.

"I do, too," Babs added.

"Otherwise," Neil said with an unmistakable sneer at the two girls, "I suppose you'll run and tattle and start trouble for me because I want to make a couple of bucks for what that guy did to me."

"We're not sneaks!" Annette's eyes flashed. "We just think you have no right to keep that thing, but we don't intend to get mixed up in it by saying anything to anybody. I only hope you don't get us all into trouble by being grabby."

Neil glowered at her. "I'm not being grabby. I just want to square things with a character who thinks he can wreck boats and have people beaten up and not pay for it." Then he added grimly, "And I'm going to do it, no matter what any of you say!"

He stowed the cylinder under the pile of diving equipment, taking special care to see that no part of it showed.

There was an uncomfortable silence as Rod raised the sail and the sloop got under way.

Neil sulked for a few minutes, but when the silence continued, he began to squirm.

"Okay," he said suddenly, startling all three. "You win. I'll take the thing up to Horton's place tomorrow morning if it's going to make so much difference to all of you. But I still can't see what harm it can do to keep the thing for a couple of days!"

"The point is," Rod told him solemnly, "it might not make any difference to you, but it might cause Horton more trouble than he can handle. Remember those two tough characters you heard taking it up with him about a bouncing check."

"Yeah," Neil agreed, "guess you're right. Well, I'll see him in the morning."

"I'm glad," Annette told him with a smile. And she reached for her ukulele and started to strum it. "How about some of that practicing we were going to do?"

11

A Broken Promise

The rest of the way back to Laguna was much more pleasant for everyone. With Neil's promise—reluctant though it had been—that he would turn over the mysterious cylinder to Tino Horton in the morning, the tension disappeared.

They planned happily for the luau and sang all the Hawaiian songs they could remember as the little boat skimmed along before a breeze that was just right for sailing.

When the sloop finally nosed in quietly beside the McCleod dock and was tied up and covered for the night, the two boys shouldered the abalone sacks and followed Annette and Babs up to the house.

It was Neil who paused on the walk to stare up the strand toward the Garrett dock. The small cruiser was there under its tarpaulin, and all was silent. The big, two-story old beach house was dark and equally silent behind its hedge.

"Thinking of going by there tonight?" Rod asked, half jokingly.

"No," Neil said sharply. "Let him worry tonight. He has that coming. I hope those two guys from Las Vegas are still on his neck, and he needs whatever is in that cylinder to get them off!"

"You haven't decided to change your mind and keep it after tonight, I hope," Rod said, worried by the tone of his friend's voice.

Neil shook his head. "Uh-uh. I told you I was taking it to Horton in the morning, and that's what I intend to do. So knock it off and let's go get this fish-cleaning business over with."

"I could use a good night's rest myself," Rod agreed as he fell into step beside Neil, and they went on up after Annette and Babs.

Both Annette and Babs shuddered as they saw the big shellfish dumped out of the sacks into the spotless sink in Aunt Lila's kitchen. But there was no use backing out now. They had wanted abalones, and now they had abalones. So they tied aprons around themselves and around Neil and Rod as well, and all four went to work, getting the mollusks ready for the luau.

It was later than any of them had planned when they finished the job and closed the refrigerator door on their neat pile of wrapped abalone steaks.

Rod and Neil helped clean up the kitchen, then yawningly headed for home while the girls climbed the stairs to their rooms and fell into bed as quickly as possible.

With only one day left before Saturday's luau, Annette had intended to be up with the birds at sunrise. But neither she nor Babs stirred till long after Aunt Lila and Uncle Archie had finished breakfast.

When she did wake up, the sun was streaming in the bedroom window and Annette knew she had overslept. She bounced out of bed and hurried to look out toward the dock. The sloop was still tied up under its tarpaulin. There was no sign of either Neil or Rod.

"They're probably both up at Tino Horton's,

having breakfast with him. I wonder if Neil had the nerve to ask him for a reward!" she said to Babs a few minutes later as she perched on the edge of her drowsy friend's bed.

Babs yawned. "He probably did, but that doesn't mean he got it."

"There must be something pretty valuable in it," Annette said soberly. "Also, maybe they're breaking the law somehow, Mr. Horton and the Marinos. I wonder if I shouldn't speak to Uncle Archie about it."

"Annette, you promised you wouldn't! Neil would be furious. The police might arrest us all as suspects. Mother would never forgive me if our name got into the paper for anything like that!" Babs was genuinely upset.

"Stop worrying," Annette told her hastily. "I gave my word I wouldn't say anything about it. I'm sorry now that I did, but I'm not going to break my promise."

"Well, it's all over now. Mr. Horton has his silly old cylinder, and he and Señor Marino can cut it in half and each take his share, for all I care! We're not even going to talk about it any more."

But it wasn't as easily dismissed as that.

They were just finishing breakfast when the doorbell rang. Aunt Lila had driven to market to buy the long list of groceries for the party and Uncle Archie had gone uptown on business, so Annette answered the ring.

The caller was Rod Lang. "Come on in," Annette told him cordially. "We still have some of those doughnuts we were too tired to eat last night."

"Thanks, but I've had breakfast," Rod said hastily. "Did Neil stop by?" He stood in the doorway.

"Why, no!" Annette shook her head.

Babs dashed into the hall. "What did Mr. Horton say when Neil asked him to pay?"

"Neil didn't," Rod said shortly. "To tell the truth, we both overslept, and when we started for Horton's place, we were too late. He was gone."

"Gone where?" Annette asked suspiciously.

"He and that man of his—Esteban, the

neighbors say his name is—had left half an hour before in the cruiser."

"For Smugglers' Cove, I suppose," Annette guessed, "to hunt for the cylinder."

"That's what we figured. I wanted to sail after them with the cylinder, but Neil pointed out that they might not have gone to Smugglers' Cove, after all, and we'd just be wasting our time. He wanted to let the whole thing slide till they got back, when he'd have a better chance to negotiate with Horton about the boat repairs."

"I suppose he thinks it's funny for them to spend probably a whole day diving for something that isn't there," Annette said angrily.

"Well, he did, sort of," Rod admitted, then hastened to add loyally, "but after a little arguing, he agreed to start out in the sloop with the cylinder just as soon as he gets back with a new sawback knife. He dropped his among the rocks last night at the cove."

"I suppose he'll want to charge Mr. Horton for that, too," Babs said with a giggle.

The phone in the den rang, and Annette

dashed to answer it. She came back a minute later. "For you, Rod. Neil's at the Scuba Club, and he sounds excited."

Rod hurried to the phone and they heard him exclaim in a shocked tone, "Three divers? Good gosh, Neil! That'll cost the guy plenty." His voice died to a murmur. He seemed to be arguing with Neil about something. Then they heard him hang up the phone with a bang. A moment later he strode in, frowning.

"Horton hired three guys from the club to dive for him at a very fancy price per hour. Neil got there a few minutes after they all left in the cruiser." Rod was obviously upset.

"You two had better dash out and give him the cylinder before they start diving," Annette advised soberly.

"I wanted to, but Neil won't go along with the idea. He says the guys will be sore at us for butting into their arrangement with Horton. Besides, he'd rather not have to let them know he's been holding out the cylinder on Horton. He feels kind of funny about it now."

"He ought to," Annette said sharply. "I think you should absolutely insist that he hand it over to Horton tonight and give up that silly idea of asking for pay for doing it."

"He's agreed to do just that," Rod said quietly. "And I intend to keep him to that agreement."

"I hope so. I'll be glad when we get rid of that thing," Annette told him gravely, and Babs agreed hastily.

A few minutes later Neil returned from the Scuba Club, looking decidedly glum. The girls and Rod had decided not to mention the cylinder unless Neil spoke about it first, but Babs and Annette couldn't help looking expectantly at him as he strode in. He scowled at them defiantly.

"Quit staring at me as if I'd committed some crime!" he snapped angrily. "I said I'd give Horton that thing tonight even if he refuses to pay the repair bills. So just forget about it." He picked up a hammer and a length of decorating bunting. "How do you want this stuff draped, Annette?"

They were all soon at work getting the

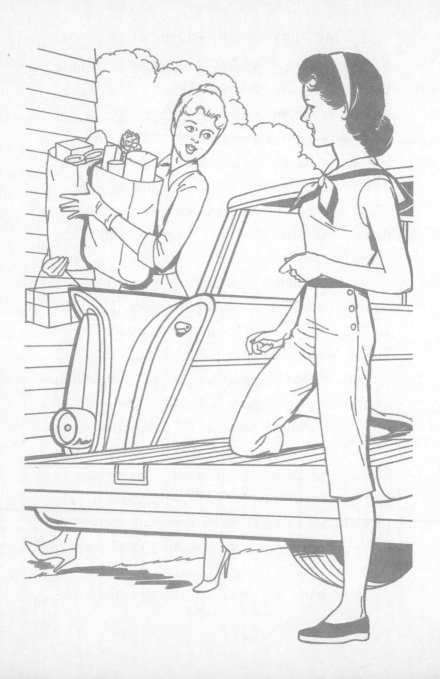

surfside patio decorated. In the midst of the preparations, Annette heard Aunt Lila's station wagon arriving, and she dashed to the garage to help unload the supplies her aunt had brought.

They made several trips into the house with the loads of food and soft drinks for the luau. It was after the last of these that Annette discovered Aunt Lila had failed to bring back one of the most important props they needed to carry out the idea of Hawaiian surroundings.

"Where are the palm branches you were supposed to get from Mrs. Whittaker's place?"

Aunt Lila looked tragic. "A dreadful thing happened, dear. Mr. Whittaker didn't know that his wife was saving them for your party and he burned up every last one of them yesterday. We'll have to think of somebody else who might have palm branches."

"But hardly anybody has palm trees around here anymore!" Annette wailed. "Of all the hard luck!" She sat on the tailgate of the station wagon and looked glum. But not for long.

"I know!" She jumped up, snapping her

fingers. "There are piles and piles of palm branches up at Smugglers' Cove!"

"But that's so far, dear," Aunt Lila said, objecting.

"I don't mind the drive, and besides, I'd like to see Señora Marino and little Pablo again. They're such nice people."

"Don't you want one of the boys to go with you to pick up the branches?"

"Oh, no. They're busy here. Besides, I think I'd like to get away by myself for a short while. There's something that's bothering me a little."

"Would you like to talk about it?" Aunt Lila asked gently. She was always ready to listen understandingly to Annette's problems, large or small.

"Oh, no, thanks, Aunt Lila! I promised—I mean—really, it's nothing important, I guess. I'm just jittery." She gave her aunt a hasty kiss and then dashed around the car to climb into the driver's seat. "Please tell the kids I'll be back before lunch and they can all help unload."

"All right, dear. Drive carefully," Aunt Lila called after her. For a moment her eyes were troubled as she watched Annette drive away. Then she smiled. Of course, the luau was probably the big problem! Some weighty matter like who would sit by whom or who would wear what. She dismissed it lightly as she went back into the house.

But Annette was not thinking about the luau as she drove toward Smugglers' Cove. She was wishing heartily she hadn't promised not to mention finding the cylinder. And she was still not sure Neil would keep his promise to Rod and herself to hand it over to Tino Horton tonight.

There was no one in the little cottage at the cove when she arrived. She was turning away to go back to the car and wait for Señora Marino to return when she heard men's voices coming faintly from the direction of the beach. Horton and the divers! she thought at once, and decided to see if they were still at work at their futile job. She felt miserably guilty and helpless, held by her promise.

She hurried down the canyon toward the beach. She was glad to see Señora Marino and Pablo there, watching the cruiser bobbing on the choppy water of the seaway. A diver was just coming aboard while a second man in a scuba outfit waited to slip overboard and continue the search. Pablo ran to meet her and led her to his grandmother. Señora Marino seemed happy to see her, and she graciously offered Annette as many of the fallen palm branches as she might need for her decorating. "Pablo and I will help you gather them," she told her. "My husband is on Tino's boat."

They went side by side up the canyon, with Pablo running happily ahead. Suddenly, the men's voices came more loudly over the water, and Señora Marino and Annette turned to look back, startled.

It was all too evident that something was wrong on the little cruiser. Señor Marino, arguing and gesturing angrily at Tino Horton, was being led forcibly by Esteban toward the railing below to which his small skiff was tied. Reluctantly, the elderly painter climbed down the ladder and boarded the skiff.

"They have quarreled again," Señora Marino said in a half whisper. "I have been afraid of this!"

12

A Change of Plans

"Something is wrong!" Señora Marino exclaimed. "I must speak to my husband. Pablo, go with the young lady to gather palm branches. I will see you later, señorita."

Without waiting for a reply from either Annette or little Pablo, Señora Marino hurried back down toward the beach to wait for her husband to row ashore.

Pablo scowled toward the cruiser out in the cove. "*Mi tío* Tino should not quarrel with my *abuelo* who is older and wiser," he said, clenching his fists.

"Oh, is Tino your uncle?" Annette asked. "Then you must be the grandson of the ex-president of San Marcos."

Pablo nodded gravely in return, "*Sí,* señorita. *El presidente* Melendez is my other *abuelo*." He held his head up proudly. "He is great and good and loved all our people very much."

Annette nodded understandingly. "That's what I read in a magazine just a few days ago. It was in a story about your uncle Tino and all the fun he's had."

Pablo frowned. "*Mi abuela*, she says we must love those who are of our own blood, but I do not love *mi tío* Tino. *Mi abuelo* says that he thinks only of himself."

Annette decided that it was best not to make any comment on Uncle Tino, but she was inclined to agree with Francisco Marino's opinion. Tino's action in swamping the sailboat and then leaving without trying to see if he had done any damage were proof enough.

They went on up the canyon, hand in hand. The palms stood high above the level of the house, and both Annette and Pablo were almost out of breath by the time they reached them. They waded through crackling masses of fallen palm branches in search of some that would be good for decoration.

Far out in the bay the divers were still at work in the underwater search. And always, of course, coming up empty-handed.

When Annette and Pablo finished gathering palm branches and had loaded them into the station wagon, they sat down on the tailgate to rest.

"Thanks a lot, Pablo," Annette said. "I don't know what we'd have done without these branches to dress up our Hawaiian luau tomorrow night."

Pablo looked wistful. "Will Mr. Rod dance? And will you sing? I should like much to be there."

"Well, I don't see why you can't come. I can pick you up tomorrow afternoon, and you can stay at my house tomorrow night after the luau. I'll bring you back here Sunday morning."

"Oh, señorita!" Pablo's black eyes danced with joy. "Let us tell *mi abuela*. Come, hurry!" He jumped off the tailgate, pulling her along with him. "I'm sure she and *mi abuelo* will have come from the beach by now."

But when they got to the little cottage, no one

was there. Pablo ran inside, calling his grand-mother, but she didn't answer. He went back to Annette.

"Perhaps they have not returned," he said, puzzled. Then he noticed that the door of the studio barn was open, and he ran back there to look for his grandparents. He disappeared inside while Annette waited.

It was Señora Marino who came out of the barn to say that Pablo was not to be allowed to go to the teenagers' party. "He is so very small, you see, Señorita Annette, and his bedtime comes very early. It would not be fair to burden yourself with the care of a little boy at your party."

"Really, I wouldn't mind," Annette said honestly.

But Señora Marino shook her head. "It is kind of you, but no." She sighed. "His grandfather is greatly troubled by a quarrel with his nephew about a certain package which was lost in the sea yesterday."

"Oh, a package?" Annette asked, feeling a guilty twinge.

"It was something of value to us all. Of great value," Señora Marino said with a sigh. "It was brought here to my husband at much risk. And now—now it is lost."

"Oh," Annette said faintly. She was tempted to say, "No, it isn't," but she remembered in time that she had given her word to Neil not to tell. Instead, she swallowed hard and managed to keep quiet.

"That is why he came out to your sailboat last night. He was hoping that your friends had found it while they were diving for the abalones."

Annette felt very uncomfortable. Maybe she should forget her promise.

But Señora Marino went on rapidly, her voice sharp with indignation, "Of course, it was not so. And my husband tried to tell Tino that there were only shellfish in the sacks which the young men brought up to the surface of the sea."

"That's true, but—" Annette began.

Señora Marino interrupted, "Of course, it is! But Tino said the young men must have tricked him somehow, for there is no trace of the package now. And he demanded that my husband tell him who the young people were."

"Did he tell?" Annette asked quickly.

"No. That is why they quarreled. My husband knows of Tino's hot temper. If he should make trouble with your friends, there might be violence. And that would mean your police would be called in and there would be investigation of certain matters. No, it is better that Tino does not know who you were."

"But if the package was for your husband, what is Tino getting so excited about?" Annette asked. But she had no sooner asked the question than she had realized what the answer was. "Oh! Of course! That bad check he gave someone at Las Vegas!"

Señora Marino looked bewildered. "What is it you are saying? A check? Las Vegas?"

Annette gulped. She hadn't meant to say that. She said quickly, "Oh, just some gossip or something that one of the boys heard. Las Vegas is a place where people gamble."

"The gossip is probably true, señorita," Señor

Marino said as he approached. "It gives me the answer that I could not find to why my nephew wishes suddenly to change plans that have been made a long time. Tell me what your friend heard." He looked stern.

"Only that your nephew was in trouble about a bad check he had given someone in Las Vegas."

"And now he seeks to pay his gambling debts with this—this package that can mean a great deal to so many of our people!" Marino said angrily. "Now I can almost hope it will never be recovered."

Annette sighed. "I guess I should tell you even if I promised not to. The boys *did* find that metal cylinder that the plane dropped. They brought it up after you had left for the shore last night, and they're planning to turn it over to Mr. Horton tonight."

"No, no!" Marino exclaimed. "They must not do that! Tino must not have it, or much harm will be done."

"If it's that important," Annette said quickly,

"I'd better try to get back home before Mr. Horton does, or I won't have a chance to stop them. They may even be waiting for him on his dock right now."

"Then go quickly, please! Tell the young men that I am waiting here for that package," Marino urged.

"I'll do better than that," Annette promised hastily. "I'll bring it back myself."

"We shall be very grateful, señorita," Señora Marino said, and her husband nodded vigorously in agreement.

Annette hurried away to her car, and the Marinos stood looking after her hopefully.

As she slowed down at the top of the hill to turn into the road that led south, Annette looked out toward Smugglers' Cove.

There was no sign of the small cruiser. Tino had evidently given up the search and gone homeward. She must hurry to get there first.

It was a bumpy road, dusty and rutted, and the station wagon was not as well upholstered as the Monster, but she gritted her teeth and bumped along as fast as she could. The palm branches bounced up and down in the back of the car.

There was a lot of early weekend traffic on the Laguna road, and Annette was forced to move more slowly than she wished. As she neared her home on the beach, she was dismayed to see Neil and a couple of the boys who were helping him go sweeping past her. They were laughing and talking, crowded into an ancient jalopy that she identified at a glance as Rod's Ol' Timer, a most unreliable mixture of car parts with cranky habits.

"Well, I won't be able to warn Neil till he gets back, but Rod's probably still hard at work fixing up things. I'll get him to give me the cylinder and then dash right back with it to the Marinos after we unload the palm branches."

But when Annette stopped the car and ran around to the beach yard, no one was there. The pit for the fire was nicely dug, however, and everything seemed under control. The fishnet decorations were in place, and abalone shells gleamed from their drapery. That was Babs's work. Looked good, too. Annette went into the house, calling Babs.

"Here we are," Babs's voice answered. Annette hurried into the big living room where Babs and Aunt Lila were stringing crepe paper into bright-colored leis. "Look at the pile we've finished," Babs said, "while you've been gone."

"Did you get the palm branches, dear?" Aunt Lila asked, looking a little harassed behind the pile of leis.

"Millions of them." Annette laughed. "Now all I need is a strong young man to unload your car and start trimming the yard with them. Where's Rod?"

"Gone to the boardinghouse to pick up a box of Hawaiian stuff he borrowed from his folks for the party," Babs explained. "And Neil is on his way to borrow one of those huge, carved wood tiki gods, the kind with the big faces. Ted Adams says no good luau is without one. You get indigestion or something from eating the feast if you don't have a tiki god set up close by where he can smell the food cooking."

"Silly," Aunt Lila said under her breath. And then, "And I want my station wagon clean inside after the young man—whoever you can get to do that much work around here—unloads it."

"Yes, Aunt Lila. I'll see to it myself," Annette promised hurriedly. "Babs, how long has Rod been gone?"

"He's been gone about ten minutes," Babs said. "He'll be right back."

"There's something I have to talk to him about," Annette told her. "Let's walk down to meet him."

"I'd love to, but we haven't finished—" Babs looked forlornly at the pile of paper in front of her.

"Oh, run along, both of you! It's time I was thinking of starting dinner, anyhow," Aunt Lila told them good-naturedly. "I'm quitting, too. We can do the rest tomorrow." She smiled at them, and they both giggled and agreed. Then they hurried out together.

Annette gave Babs a hasty rundown on the situation as they hurried along the beach walk toward the boardinghouse.

"So you see," she concluded, "why I have to keep Neil from trying to bargain with Mr. Horton for that cylinder. It isn't really Mr. Horton's property at all."

"It's too mysterious for me," Babs said with a yawn. "I only hope Neil doesn't get too stubborn."

"Me, too," Annette agreed. "But I guess Rod will be able to make him listen to reason. He sometimes can."

They were almost at the door of the boarding-house before they noticed that the cruiser was parked at the dock in front of the Garrett place. It was apparently berthed for the night, covered with its canvas.

"Oh, dear!" Babs exclaimed. "It looks as if Mr. Horton's been home for quite a while."

Annette frowned. "He must have given up and pulled out of the cove right after Señor Marino rowed ashore. I only hope Rod and Neil haven't discovered he's back and turned that cylinder over to him!"

"We'll know in just a minute," Babs agreed

grimly. They hurried to knock on the boarding-house door. Just as they were knocking, the door opened and a large pasteboard box started out. The legs that were supporting it looked familiar in Rod's beige pants.

"Hey! Look where you're going!" Annette laughed. Rod peered at them around the corner of the box.

"Hi, kids! Wait till you see the big conch shell we'll blow tomorrow night to announce that the luau is about to start! And the colored-glass floats—all sizes, and—" Rod set down the huge box as Annette interrupted.

"Sounds swell," she said hastily, "but what we're here for is the cylinder!"

"Why, I haven't got it. Neil has!" Rod said.

The two girls looked at each other and groaned. Maybe Neil had already turned it over to Horton!

13

Hide-and-seek

"What's wrong with you two? Why the groans?" Rod asked.

"That cylinder was supposed to be delivered to Señor Marino, and I've promised him that I'll bring it to him tonight. Now maybe Neil has handed it over to Mr. Horton!" Annette moaned.

"I'm sure he hasn't," Rod insisted. "Neil and I are going up there together with it after Neil gets the tiki set up in your yard, and the other kids have gone home."

"Thank goodness!" Babs rolled her eyes.

"Then where's the cylinder now? In his room?" Annette asked eagerly. "Will you get it for us?"

Rod frowned and shook his head. "It's not in his room. He has it tucked away at your uncle's place."

"Then let's go get it while I fill you in on what the Marinos told me," Annette said briskly.

"I don't know about taking it," Rod said, objecting. "Neil will be sore. He still figures on asking Tino Horton to pay for the repair of the sailboat in return for the cylinder."

But after Annette had told him what the Marinos had said about the missing cylinder's meaning so much to so many people, Rod decided she was right to want to give it to them instead of to Horton. "But Neil won't like it. You'll have to argue to get the thing away from him."

"I'll be glad to," Annette said grimly. "He had no right keeping it in the first place."

Rod looked guilty. "I guess it was a pretty juvenile stunt we did. I'm glad you found out who really owns whatever is in the cylinder before we delivered it to Horton."

"Thank goodness Annette got back before that happened. Once Mr. Horton had it, that would have been the end," Babs agreed. "But he *is* awfully cute."

"Ugh," Annette said with a reproachful look

at her friend. Then she turned to Rod. "Let's go."

"Okay, but I think we ought to wait till Neil comes back before we take the thing. At least we should tell him why you think it's the right thing to do."

"Fair enough," Annette agreed.

"Then grab some of these heavy shells out of this box, and, Babs, you carry a few of these Japanese glass fishing floats for me, so I won't collapse under the weight of all this!" Without waiting for them to agree, Rod piled the big shells and the colored globes into their arms in spite of Babs's groans. Then he poised the considerably lighter carton on his head and led the way down the walk, singing and doing some fancy steps to the tune of "Waikiki Beach Boy."

They laughed at his antics and balanced the heavy shells and floats precariously as they followed him. For the first time in hours, Annette felt lighthearted. In just a few minutes she would have the mysterious cylinder. Then, after dinner, she and Babs could dash out to Smugglers' Cove in the Monster and deliver it to the worried

Marinos. And that would be the last of it as far as she and her friends were concerned.

There was no sign of Neil as they arrived in the McCleod front yard, but a tall, carved wood tiki stood alongside the fire pit, its huge, grotesque features looking very menacing.

"Hiya, Teek, old boy!" Rod saluted it. "We bring offerings and all that sort of stuff!" He bowed, then gaily dumped the remaining contents of the carton on the sand at the foot of the idol.

Babs shivered. "Goodness! Better be respectful or he'll see to it that we all have indigestion tomorrow night!"

Rod laughed, but a moment later he glanced at Annette and saw she wasn't smiling. He sobered at once. "Neil will be along soon, Annette," he assured her quickly. "He's probably putting away my car and saying good night to the guys who helped him bring our friend here."

"Do you know where he might have left the cylinder?" Annette asked, looking around hopefully. "It won't do any harm to get it out while we're waiting for him."

"Might be under that pile of bunting we had left over," Rod suggested.

The girls hurried after him and helped remove the discarded lengths of red, white, and blue bunting heaped in the corner. There was nothing under it but the sand.

"Guess again, Rod," Babs said, sneezing from the dust covering the bunting.

But Annette was looking closely at the sand where the bunting had been piled. "It *was* here," she told them quickly, pointing to a deep impression in the sand, "but he must have taken it away again."

"Well," Rod said grimly, "that seems to be that!"

"I suppose he decided not to wait for you to go with him," Annette said, frowning. "But if he's on his way to Horton's, we would have met him on the walk."

"Yeah, that's right," Rod agreed, brightening. "Maybe he simply decided to hide it somewhere else safer. All we have to do is find him and ask."

"Find who?" It was Neil's voice. They all

looked toward the rear door of the garage. "Who is it you're hunting?"

"You, bud, just you!" Rod laughed. "We were wondering where you stashed a certain package when you moved it from under that bunting."

"What's all the steam about?" Neil's voice sounded sullen and unfriendly. "I've got it okay."

"Wow! What a relief!" Annette said fervently.

"What are you talking about?" Neil stood over them, scowling.

"Tell him what's happened, Annette," Rod said quietly.

So Annette told him about the Marinos and her promise to deliver the mysterious cylinder to them. Neil was very quiet as she spoke, but when she was through, he announced firmly that he still intended to give the thing to Horton and try to get the cost of the sailboat repairs out of him.

"But you can't!" Annette said impatiently.

"Annette's right. I'm on her side," Rod told his friend.

But it took another five minutes of three-against-one arguing before Neil would give in. Finally he said, "Okay, then. But there's something I ought to tell you—" He swallowed hard a couple of times and then got it out. "You'd better take a look at it first."

They exchanged puzzled glances as Neil led the way to Uncle Archie's workshop next to the garage.

The cylinder was lying on the workbench, empty.

"What happened? Where's the stuff that was in it?" Rod demanded.

"Where's the money or jewelry or whatever it was?" Annette asked at the same time. "Did Mr. Horton find it and grab it?"

"There wasn't any money or jewelry," Neil said with a scowl, "and Horton doesn't even know I've got the thing."

"Well, who opened it then?" Annette flashed angrily. "One of your goofy friends who've been helping us here?"

"No!" Neil snapped. "I just got to thinking about what might be in it, and I thought I'd take a look. One of the seals here at the end looked loose, so I pried it off and—well, the end kind of came off, I guess."

"So you dumped out the stuff and had a good look," Rod said grimly. "Where is it now?"

"The only 'stuff' in it was this old, dark-looking painting. Just junk as far as I can see," Neil said, turning to the workbench to pick up a roll of canvas that looked brown with age.

"It certainly seems old," Annette said, helping Rod spread the canvas on the worktable. "But the colors of the clothing are vivid, though the people look eight feet tall. That angel over on the side, for instance."

"Yeah," Neil agreed. "He'd never get off the ground with a wingspread like that!"

"I don't see why everyone's making such a fuss over an old thing like this," Babs said scornfully.

"Because it must be worth a lot of money," Annette said soberly, "even if it's all cracked and faded in spots."

"It doesn't look like ready money to *me*," Neil said.

"And we thought there'd be money or jewelry or something exciting like that in the cylinder!" Babs complained.

Neil snorted suddenly, looking worried. "Yipes! I bet I know what's happened here! There's been a fast switch. Somebody's looted the money stuff out of the cylinder along the way here to old Marino. This other junk was probably in somebody's attic, and they just stuffed it in so it would weigh the same as the original load."

"I suppose that could have happened, but I still think this painting could be worth a lot," Rod said quietly.

"And *I* say this thing is just junk," Neil answered stubbornly.

"I think Neil's right," Babs said. "Somebody must've stolen the contents. I hope when Señor Marino sees that you opened the cylinder, he won't think it was you who took whatever was in it!" She turned wide-eyed to Neil.

"Gosh! So he might!" Neil looked panicky. "Horton will be sure to think so, too. I wish I'd kept my nose out of the thing now!" He looked appealingly at Rod. "What are we going to do now?"

"Personally, I think you're getting excited over nothing," Rod told him gravely, "but there is an outside chance you're right about the switch." He turned to Annette. "What do you think, Annette?"

She shook her head firmly. "I think this painting is what Señor Marino is expecting. It's very old and it's probably worth a fortune. But—" she hesitated, "if Neil is so worried, why don't we try to put it back into the cylinder and seal it up again? Could we, Rod?"

Rod frowned uncertainly, looking at the cylinder and the cap that Neil had pried off. "I suppose so, if we had the tools, solder, and stuff."

Neil brightened at once. "Do you think so?"

Rod nodded. "I think I could fix it so nobody would notice it had been opened."

"Thank goodness!" Babs exclaimed, giving Annette an enthusiastic hug. "I could just see Mom's face if there was a row, and it got into the papers that we were mixed up in stealing those jewels or money or whatever!"

"First thing is to get it back into the cylinder very carefully," Rod told Neil. "Annette, do you know where your uncle keeps his soldering iron?"

"It should be right here in among his tools. What would it look like?" Annette asked, hurrying to the tool cabinet.

Rod gave her a quick description, and she and Babs began looking. But a soldering iron seemed to be one of the few tools that Uncle Archie didn't have in his beach workshop.

They were still looking for it when they heard a horn honking in the driveway.

Then there were calls of "Annette! Where are you?" Annette recognized the voice of Lisa Kerry, her very closest friend at school and one of tomorrow night's guests of honor.

The painting was safely in the cylinder now, and Annette told Rod hastily, "Let's put it out of sight. It sounds as if Lisa has the whole gang with her. No use advertising what's going on."

"Right!" Rod agreed. He slid the cylinder into the bottom drawer of the cabinet beside him.

"Don't worry. I'll take care of the soldering job. I know a guy down the road who has all kinds of tools. When Lisa and the other kids leave, I'll dash down to his place and borrow the equipment. I can start on the job first thing in the morning."

"Wonderful!" Annette cried. She felt sure that she'd be on her way out to the Marinos' bright and early to get rid of the cylinder for good.

They closed the door on the workshop and hurried to give a hearty welcome to the carful of teenagers who had arrived with Lisa.

14

Delays and Dangers

Annette was so happy to see Lisa Kerry and Jinks and the others that she almost forgot about the troublesome cylinder. Everyone had to tell the others what he or she had been doing during the long vacation, and the house was filled with excited chatter.

It was several hours before they left, all of them eager to come to tomorrow night's luau and brimming over with plans for their costumes. Most of the girls planned to make their own muumuus, while the boys favored sarongs, tattered beachcomber outfits, or rugged sailor pants for their costumes.

Rod was the last to leave. He waited till Aunt Lila was out of hearing and then told Annette, "I called the fellow who has a soldering iron, and he'll let me borrow it tomorrow morning. I'm hoping the job won't take long, once I get the hang of it. Check with me in the workshop about nine-thirty in the morning."

"You're swell!" Annette told him, and she stopped worrying.

In the morning, however, it was Neil whom she found in her uncle's workshop instead of Rod. He was loafing and reading the morning paper.

"Oh, hi," she greeted him. "Where did Rod put 'the Thing' when he finished it? How does it look?"

"Looks same as it did before. Wide-open," Neil said gloomily. "It's still in the drawer. The soldering iron had a short in it. Rod's out now, trying to scare up another one."

"Oh, dear! I was hoping I could dash over to the Marinos' right away. I know they must be wondering why I didn't bring it back yesterday as I promised." She held up a colorful paper lei to show him. "I'm taking Pablo a souvenir of the luau."

"He's not at the cove. He's here, at his uncle's.

Rod and I saw Horton marching him up from the dock this morning, not an hour ago. He had the kid by the hand, and the kid was trying to pull loose but couldn't make it."

"I can't believe it! Pablo with his uncle? I can't imagine his grandparents' letting Tino Horton take him anywhere. Especially after the argument yesterday!"

Neil shrugged. "Maybe the kid begged to come. He was keen to watch the luau, you said."

Annette nodded. "Yes, but Pablo dislikes his uncle so much, I'm sure he'd never willingly go anywhere with him. You say he was trying to break away from Horton?"

"Well, that's how it looked, anyhow." Neil yawned. "Maybe he just didn't like being led along by the hand like an infant."

"Or maybe Horton just snatched him up and brought him away from his grandparents without asking them if he could. But I wonder why he would do that?" Annette was puzzled.

"Maybe out of spite," Neil suggested. Rod spoke up from the doorway. "Uh-uh," he said, shaking his head and looking grim. "I have a hunch he was trying to find out who was abalone fishing the other night in the cove. And Pablo had the answers and wouldn't know he wasn't supposed to tell his uncle. So Horton got him onto the cruiser somehow and tricked him into telling who we were!"

"Why do you think that?" Annette asked, wide-eyed.

"Because somebody just ransacked our rooms at the boardinghouse looking for something. Polkie heard noises up there and went to investigate. But the guy got away without her seeing who it was."

Neil was alarmed. "What did he take?"

"Nothing. He passed up that eight bucks in my cuff-link box and your gold watch lying on your dresser. So he wasn't looking for cash or stuff to pawn. I feel sure it was either Horton or that hardfisted thug that works for him looking for the cylinder."

"Did Polkie call the police?" Annette was worried.

Rod shook his head. "I talked her out of it. Told her it was probably one of the scuba guys looking for that equipment we borrowed. Boy, I'll be glad when this cylinder thing is off our hands for good."

"Me, too," Annette admitted glumly.

Neil nodded vigorous agreement.

Aunt Lila's voice came from the direction of the beach patio. "Annette!"

"Oops! Got to go," she said hastily. "Can you finish the soldering before lunch? I told Aunt Lila I had one more errand to do before I could settle down and help get ready for the luau, but I had to be back by one."

"I'll do my best," Rod promised. "The main worry is to fix the cylinder carefully so it won't show the seals have ever been broken. I'll have to dull down the solder, and—"

Annette interrupted. "Okay, Rod. I know you'll hurry as much as you can. If I can't get out to the Marinos' with it this morning, I'll just have to take it out tonight, after the luau is over. I know the Marinos must be terribly worried about Pablo. They may not know Horton has him. They may even think he's drowned!"

She hurried away to find her aunt and learn what her aunt wished to have done first. She was just in time to hear Aunt Lila talking on the phone.

"Oh, yes, Mr. Horton, I'm sure my brother will be most interested in your photographs of the big-game fishing. He'll be home all evening if you care to drop in. The young people are having a Hawaiian luau—" She broke off and chuckled as she listened.

"Now what's he up to?" Annette asked herself, and she lingered for a clue while Aunt Lila chatted.

"You haven't?" Aunt Lila was surprised. "Well, I'm sure my niece and her friends would be flattered to have you watch them singing those funny little Hawaiian songs that have dances to go with them. And you might find it amusing. You will come? Good!"

Annette waited a minute more, expecting to hear Pablo mentioned, but Aunt Lila hung up the phone almost at once and bustled away busily.

So Horton would be around tonight, in all the excitement of the party. He probably thought it would be a good chance for Esteban or himself to go snooping for the cylinder, Annette thought. Well, he was going to be disappointed. She intended to get the sealed cylinder safely to the Marinos, even if she had to leave the luau before the party was half over!

The rest of the day both Annette and Babs were too busy even to think of the mysterious cylinder. There were a dozen things to do before the guests were due to arrive at sundown.

A full moon would be rising at almost the same moment that sunset darkened into twilight, adding a touch of glamour to the scene. That was when the tiki torches would blaze at the corners of the beach patio, and the chattering guests in their long-skirted muumuus would gather with their escorts in South Sea Island calico sarongs, then take their places around the long, low, board table attractively decorated with flowers and bowls of fruit.

The fire pit, or *imu*, while not exactly

Hawaiian in appearance, was a good enough substitute. Uncle Archie had given reluctant permission to sink the iron bowl of the barbecue brazier in the sand and build the cooking fire in it. It was quite effective as Neil hovered over it importantly, posing in a bright-colored print for the earliest guests to snap pictures of him.

Annette, almost finished with her many tasks, dabbed on a final bit of powder, put a hibiscus flower in her hair, and dashed out to the festive table with the last big tray of appetizers.

A glimpse of Neil reminded her that she hadn't seen Rod for the last couple of hours, not since he had popped into the kitchen where she and Aunt Lila were working. He had grinned, made an okay sign to her, and then dashed away again.

Now he was nowhere in sight in the patio. She thought he might at least have told her where he had put the cylinder before he disappeared. But maybe it was back in the cabinet drawer again. She decided to check.

The workshop door was open a few inches,

and she switched on the light as she went in. Rod was sitting on the floor, holding his jaw and groaning. He blinked painfully and asked, "Gosh, what time is it?"

"What happened?" Annette hurried to him.

"I came in here right after I saw you in the kitchen, to get the soldering iron and take it back to Bill Tracy. Somebody was behind the door and jumped me. I didn't get a look at him, but I can guess who it was." He felt his jaw gingerly and looked at the tools scattered around and the cabinet drawers hanging open.

"So can I," Annette agreed glumly. "Did they get—'the Thing'?"

"Nope!" He managed a faint chuckle. "I out-foxed 'em. It wasn't here."

"Where is it?"

"The Monster's taking care of it for us." He grinned.

"That's good!" Annette was relieved. "That'll make it easy for me when—" She broke off abruptly at the sound of hurried footsteps near the doorway.

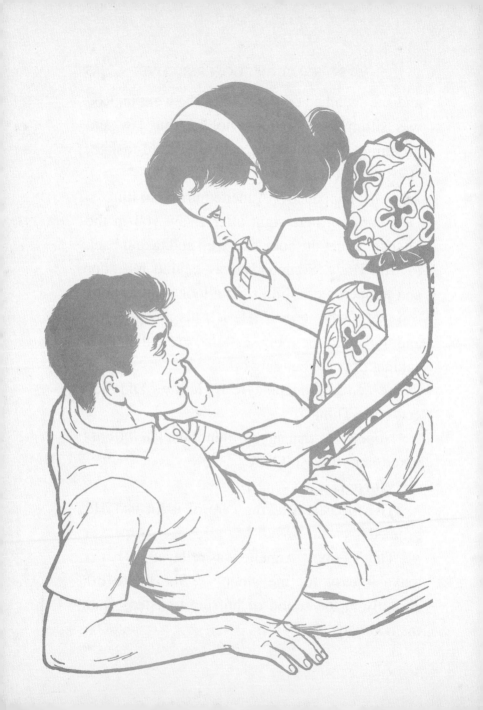

Rod strode hastily to the door and looked out, but there was no one in sight. A group of guests was approaching from one of the parked cars and they yelled greetings to Rod. He had to wait to say hello and wasn't able to dash around the corner and see who had just been hovering outside the workshop.

"That could have been Horton or Esteban listening to us," Annette told Rod as they hurried to meet the guests. "If it was, now they know where we have the cylinder."

Rod waved it away reassuringly. "Quit being jittery. They'd have no idea what we meant by the Monster."

"Maybe not, but they could ask any of the kids and find out. I think I'll slip away just as soon as Babs and you start your hula lesson number. The kids will be having a ball trying to hula, and half of them won't miss me. I'll get back before they notice I've been away."

A little later, while the fun and feasting were at their height and Rod was doing his beachboy number, Annette noticed Tino Horton standing back at the edge of the torchlit patio with her uncle. They were both watching Rod and laughing at his antics.

There was no sign of Esteban or of little Pablo. His uncle probably ordered the poor little fellow to bed and left that gorilla Esteban watching him, she thought with indignation. Pablo had wanted so much to see the luau.

She had a sudden idea. If she could talk to Pablo and find out if he was all right, she would be able to reassure his grandparents when she gave them the cylinder. Of course, maybe she was figuring wrongly. Maybe they knew where he was; maybe he was merely visiting his uncle. But somehow, she didn't believe it. She decided to try to see him right away if she could manage it.

She and Babs were supposed to do a duet in a few minutes, but she hoped Babs would be willing to do it alone.

She hurried to the makeshift dressing room at the edge of the patio. Babs was busy adding touches to her makeup, and she squealed with dismay when Annette told her hastily that she would have to go solo.

"I'd be petrified! I can't do it!" she told Annette. "You're the one who really dances. I just follow what you do. Please, Annette, let that horrid old cylinder and that little boy stay just where they are tonight!"

"I can't, Babs," Annette told her. "I have a feeling—"

"Where is that pesty cylinder now?" Babs pouted.

"In the Monster safe and sound for the moment," Annette said grimly, "but we don't know how long it will stay that way." And she quickly explained about the eavesdropper outside the workshop.

Babs interrupted excitedly. "Oh, you'd better hurry! I saw that man Esteban talking to a couple of the kids not five minutes ago, and I'm sure I heard Jinks Bradley say something about the Monster and laugh!"

"That does it!" Annette told her hastily and started away. At the doorway she stopped a moment. "Just keep thinking that none of the kids knows any more about the hula than you do, and if you forget what we rehearsed, make up something. And remember to wriggle your hands and don't move your feet too much!" Then she was gone.

Annette went into the garage through the rear door and was just about to unlock the door to the driveway when she heard someone outside rattling the lock. A moment later, there was a sound of hammering, like rock on metal.

Someone was trying to break the lock. Annette waited, trying to decide what to do.

"Hey, there, guy!" It was Neil's voice. "Cut that out! Whaddya think you're doing, you big ape?" She could hear Neil running up to the door, then the sound of blows and a struggle. She heard Neil's voice again, but now it was a little out of breath from the battle. "This time, bud, it's my turn!" The sound of a crash came, then a couple of groans.

Annette had to look. If Neil had gotten the worst of it, maybe she could help. She quietly unlocked and noiselessly slid up the heavy door, a chunk of firewood ready in her hand. But it was Neil who was on his feet and his opponent who was stretched out unconscious. Just as she had suspected, it was Esteban.

"Hi! Neat work! Thanks a million!" Annette told Neil. "I almost ran into him."

"He won't get in your way for quite a while," Neil assured her. "He's out cold. I really landed one on him after he tried to brain me with that rock!"

"Would I have time to run up to the Garrett place and talk to Pablo?" she asked quickly.

"Help yourself," Neil told her. "I'll just baby-sit with this little fellow and see that nothing disturbs his nap while you're gone. If he starts waking up, I'll give him a nice li'l sleeping pill." He grinned and doubled his fist menacingly.

"Okay," Annette said with a laugh. "I'll make it quick." And she started hurriedly up the strand to disappear into the darkness.

15

Clearing Skies

The big house on the strand was dark except for a dim light in a second-story window. There, a small shadow moved about behind the thin bedroom curtain, and Annette felt certain it was Pablo's.

There might be servants guarding Pablo, so she couldn't venture boldly inside. Instead, she tossed pebbles lightly against the second-story window. After only a few throws, she was rewarded by seeing Pablo part the curtain and look down.

She stood back in the bright moonlight and motioned. After a moment, the boy softly opened the window.

"Pablo! Do you want to go home?" she called softly.

That was all Pablo needed. He was out of the

window and climbing over the porch rail in half a minute. She caught him as he dropped into the bushes, and he clung to her, sobbing.

"I am so happy you came for me, señorita," he said. "*Mi tío* says he will take me far away to punish *mi abuelo* because he will not tell him something which he wishes to know. He asks me many questions, and some I try to answer so he will let me go home. But I am afraid of him and Esteban."

"Well, you're going to forget about both of them from now on," Annette assured him grimly. "We're leaving for Smugglers' Cove right now."

They ran back to Annette's house hand in hand. Pablo became more excited by the minute as they heard the sounds of the party more clearly.

"Please, señorita, may I watch the dancing for just one small minute?" he begged, breathlessly.

"I'm sorry, Pablo. It wouldn't be safe," Annette told him. "We might be seen by your uncle or Esteban."

"Oh," he said disappointedly, and let her lead him to the driveway behind the garage.

She was happy to see that Esteban was still sleeping and Neil, the baby-sitter, was still on guard. Neil grinned at the sight of her and Pablo. "Only had to give him one extra tap a minute ago," he confided happily. "But you'd better start for the cove before anybody comes looking for Baby." He nodded toward Esteban.

"Right!" Annette agreed, and she hurried toward the white sports car. "Come along, Pablo," she called back over her shoulder. Then she stopped suddenly. Pablo was not following her. He wasn't anywhere in sight. "Where is he?" she asked Neil sharply.

Neil shrugged. "I dunno. Just disappeared. Probably wants to see the fun."

Annette felt her heart sink. "I'll get him back. If his uncle sees him—" She left it unsaid and hurried away toward the beach patio.

Rod and Babs were conducting a noisy and gleeful class of would-be hula dancers of both sexes up on the performing platform at the end of the patio. The record player was at its loudest in a lively Hawaiian hula, and the guests seated around on the mats were hilarious with laughter at the dancers.

Annette looked hastily for Pablo and finally spotted him at the far edge of the platform. He was looking on, fascinated. She took a hurried step toward him and then stopped abruptly as a hand closed tightly on her arm, and Tino Horton loomed up beside her. His face was stern and threatening, but his voice was soft as he said smoothly, "Ah, Señorita Annette! How pleasant at last to meet you face-to-face! Shall we take a small walk out to your garage? I believe you have something there that belongs to me."

As Horton spoke, he tightened his grip cruelly on Annette's arm and began to lead her firmly toward the palm-decked exit.

For a moment she was too startled to resist, and she went along with him. Up on the platform the amateur hula dancers stopped gyrating as the record ended. Rod dashed to start it over.

"Hold it, kids!" Rod called, then turned to the audience. "Last call for wigglers! Come on, join the party!"

Annette stopped abruptly, in spite of the hard pressure on her arm, and called out loudly, "Here, Rod! Got one for you!" Then cheerfully, "Come on, Mr. Horton! Don't be afraid to try!" She wrenched free, grabbed his arm, and started to pull him toward the platform. "Come on, gang! Here's a bashful one! Give me a hand!"

After his first surprise, Horton tried to hold back. But Rod had jumped from the platform and he ran to help Annette drag him to the stage. The others, all in fun, lent their help, pushing and dragging the angry man. In a moment they had pulled him up on the platform.

"Hold him, girls, or he'll run away!" Annette called playfully. "How about some leis for Mr. Horton?"

They responded by mobbing Horton laughingly, draping leis around his neck, holding onto him when he tried to duck and get away. He didn't have a chance. Finally he stopped struggling and tried to laugh with them.

"Keep him here, Babs!" Annette whispered hastily. Babs got a firm hold on Horton as the music started, and she laughingly insisted on teaching him how to do the steps.

Annette slipped away to Pablo, who was watching openmouthed and puzzled. "Come! We are going now!" she told him, taking his hand and hurriedly leading him out toward the garage.

They were just disappearing when Horton noticed they were leaving. He shoved Babs aside so hard that she tripped and nearly fell. He ignored her and dashed for the edge of the platform.

"Hold it, bud!" Rod barked, barring his way. "You can't get rough around here!"

But Horton pushed him violently aside and jumped down. Before Rod regained his balance, Horton was gone.

The dancers were milling about, Babs was tearfully denouncing Horton, and there was complete bedlam. Rod had no chance to follow Horton for a couple of minutes.

In the garage, Annette was quickly backing her car out when Horton ran in from the patio. Neil's attention was on Esteban, who had staggered to his feet at the sound of the car starting

up. The two men were wrestling, with Esteban trying to get to Annette and Neil trying to stop him.

Horton made a wild leap to grab the car door and reach the ignition to turn it off. Annette made a fast swing with the obedient Monster, and Horton missed his grasp and sprawled.

A second later, Annette was speeding away on the long trip to Smugglers' Cove.

Horton scrambled to his feet and glared after the disappearing car. His own rented car was in the Garrett garage. There was another car in the McCleod garage—Aunt Lila's station wagon. He ran to it.

His luck was good. As usual she had left her keys in it. He started the motor.

The sound of a second car startled Neil. He looked over his shoulder just long enough for Esteban to land a punch that floored him. Then Horton was joined by Esteban in the station wagon, and they roared out. A moment later, Rod ran in to find out what had been happening.

It was doubtful whether Rod's Ol' Timer

could overtake the station wagon, but the boys knew they had to try anyway.

By the time Uncle Archie had hurried out to see what all the gunning of motors was about, the boys were on their way at Ol' Timer's best speed.

Annette sped along the beach highway. She had no way of knowing which, if any, of the lights reflected in her rearview mirror were from a pursuing car. All she could do was drive as fast as possible. She dreaded the last long stretch of abandoned road along the hills where she would have to slow down.

Pablo was tense and silent at her side, looking back nervously from time to time. "We'll soon be there," she told him cheerfully as she turned off into the long, hilly stretch of the old road.

But now the many reflections in her mirror had settled down to one. And it seemed to be coming closer, although she pressed down hard on the accelerator and the Monster roared ahead over the bumpy road.

Now the ups and downs of the hill road hid the headlights of the pursuing car from time to time, but they always appeared again.

She sent the Monster up a steep hill at top speed and roared down the other side, then along the last stretch of the old highway to the place where the dirt road turned down into Smugglers' Cove. It was a rough, jolting ride.

With a squeal of brakes, she brought the sports car to a stop and turned off her lights. In the stillness of the moonlit night, she sat gripping Pablo's hand and listening tensely. They heard the soft pounding of the surf in the cove, but there was no sound from the pursuing car.

Maybe they couldn't get up the hill—or the going was too bumpy, she thought happily.

Pablo stared back, his eyes like saucers. "D-did we lose them, señorita?"

"Looks like it, hon," Annette told him happily. "Let's unload and get down to your grandfather's house." She jumped out and dug the cylinder from under a pile of torn bunting and old newspapers in the rear of the car. "Be careful with it now," she warned Pablo. "Your grandfather says it's very valuable."

"*Sí,* señorita, I know!" Pablo grinned widely. He took one end and Annette took the other, and they started down the hill path, hurrying as much as they dared.

When they were still only halfway to the house, they heard a car on the road above and saw the loom of its lights against the sky.

Annette and Pablo moved quickly into the brush alongside the road and crouched there a moment, trying to decide what to do. Up above, the lights were turned off on the car, and they could hear a murmur of men's voices.

"Is it my *tío* Tino?" Pablo whispered with a shiver.

Annette nodded. "I'm afraid so. You'd better run down and tell your grandfather I have his package here and I'll hide with it till I see your uncle leave."

"*Sí!*" Pablo took off rapidly down the dirt road and disappeared into the darkness.

Annette heard footsteps above. There were people coming down the road. She saw them silhouetted against the sky and felt panic. One was big and broad-shouldered, one slim and wiry. Then, as they came closer, she heard the slim one laugh.

"Well, that takes care of Mr. Tino Horton for a few days!" It was Rod.

She stood up abruptly and called, "Rod! Neil! Oh, I'm so glad it's you!" She hurried toward them dragging the cylinder with her. Both boys ran to meet her, and Rod put his arm around her to steady her as she held onto both of them, almost in tears. "I was afraid Horton had caught up with us."

"He won't catch up with anybody for a few days, if your uncle has anything to say about it. He found out somebody had stolen your aunt's station wagon and called the sheriff. The highway patrol picked up Mr. Horton and his friend Esteban doing seventy back there a few miles. So he's in jail with a whole ticketful of charges, including resisting arrest. And Esteban's right with him." Neil chuckled happily.

"What a relief!" Annette laughed. Then they went to the Marinos' cottage, Neil a little solemn as he carried the metal-enclosed painting on his shoulder.

Neil still had to explain that even though he had been curious enough to break into the cylinder, he had not stolen its contents and replaced them with the worthless painting it now contained.

But Neil was in for a surprise, and Annette and Rod were able to smile just a little smugly at each other, as they watched Francisco Marino reverently remove the faded painting from its metal case. He smiled proudly as he spread it gently on his worktable. "It is here at last! The work of the great master El Greco. The most valuable possession of my family for four hundred years!"

"Valuable? But it's all faded over here on the edge, and it's dark in spots and cracked," Neil protested in disbelief. "You mean it's worth real money?"

"A great deal," Marino assured him happily. "It is a regret that we must lose it from the family, but the money it will bring to our exiled countrymen will furnish food and shelter for a long time to many who need it badly."

"There's only one thing I was wondering

about," Annette said gravely. "I always thought antiques like this were admitted duty-free. Why did it have to be sort of—uh—sneaked in—smuggled, I mean?"

Marino smiled. "It was not a question of evading the tax, but rather of getting it safely out of San Pascual and keeping it out of the hands of the revolutionary government of our own poor country. They learned through spies that my brother planned to ship it to me in order to sell it to a famous gallery in New York, which has already offered a large sum for it. It was necessary to remove it secretly before they could send a raiding party across the border to seize it for themselves. Tomorrow I shall make an early call at your customs house with this, then ship it at once to New York. After that, I shall see what I can do to help my misguided nephew out of his troubles with your local laws and with the gamblers!"

"We'll be glad to chauffeur you anywhere you want to go on Monday, Señor Marino." Neil beamed at him. The big fellow was happily relieved now that he would not have to admit that he had snooped into the cylinder. The world was right again.

Señora Marino urged them to stay for chocolate and *bizcochitos*, but Annette told her that they had to get back to the luau as soon as they could. Then, with a hearty hug for Pablo and a promise to come again soon, Annette and the boys hurried back to the party.

It was still going on when they drove up, and they laughingly refused to tell where they had been. But no one cared much—they were all having too much fun. Only Babs pouted a little because she hadn't been in on all the excitement. She soon recovered, however, and went back to hold hands with an "awfully cute" new boy who was going to be in some of her classes the next term.

Annette and the boys had agreed not to burden Uncle Archie and Aunt Lila with all the details of the business about the cylinder and about Tino Horton.

Without actually saying so, Annette let them

keep the impression that Mr. Horton borrowed the car as a joke on herself and all her friends to pay them back for dragging him into the hula line. So when Monday came, Uncle Archie had dropped the charges against young Tino Horton. And shortly thereafter, the Garrett house was empty, and Tino had moved out of their lives.

It was the day before the McCleods closed the beach house for the summer that Annette went back to the cove.

She found the Marinos packing to return to San Marcos. A counterrevolution by the old regime had been a success, and all was peace and happiness in the little country once more.

They made her promise to come to see them someday, and Annette agreed to write often. Pablo wept at the last minute and had to run and hide, and her own eyes were misty as she waved good-bye and started on her way back to Laguna.

She did not want to come back to Smugglers' Cove again for a long time, she thought to herself, but she knew that she would never forget her exciting experiences there.